LISA HUGHES realized too late what a wonderful man her first husband was. Now Bob Hughes didn't want any part of her. Could she make up for all the pain she'd caused him and rekindle the fire of passion?

DONALD HUGHES felt intoxicated by the mere presence of Lisa in his life. He knew his family was right; she was no good for him. Could he resist her fatal charms long enough to see what he was getting himself into?

JENNIFER RYAN felt torn between her love for her son and her commitment to Bob Hughes. Her life was so empty without Bob. Wasn't there a way she could make Rick understand her desperate need?

———————————

Series Story Editor **Mary Ann Cooper** is America's foremost soap opera expert. She writes the nationally syndicated column *Speaking of Soaps*, is a major contributor to soap opera magazines, and has appeared on numerous radio and television talk shows.

Sonni Cooper, author of *Forbidden Passions*, is an experienced script writer from the west coast. Her most recent novel, entitled *Black Fire*, has become a favorite among science fiction fans across the country.

Dear Friend,

Lisa Hughes is the type of female most women envy. Beautiful and sexy, she knows how to get what she wants. It seems only natural that the Hughes family would be wary of her. Bob Hughes once fell head over heels for her, and it nearly destroyed him.

In book 5 of AS THE WORLD TURNS, Lisa sets her sights on Bob's brother, Donald. Chris and Nancy Hughes can't help but feel a sense of doom. An entanglement with Lisa is an experience they don't wish to repeat.

At Pioneer Communications Network, Inc., repetition is our sincerest form of flattery. We believe that reliving soap opera stories from the past not only enriches today's viewing pleasure, but also provides exciting, entertaining reading. As the publishers of Soaps & Serials paperback books, we take great pride in fulfilling that goal, month after month.

For Soaps & Serials books,

Mary Ann Cooper

Mary Ann Cooper

P.S. If you missed previous AS THE WORLD TURNS books and can't find them in your local book source, please see the order form inserted in the back of this book.

AS THE WORLD TURNS

5

Forbidden Passions

PIONEER COMMUNICATIONS NETWORK, INC.

Forbidden Passions

AS THE WORLD TURNS paperback novels are
published and distributed by Pioneer Communications
Network, Inc.

SOAPS & SERIALS™ is a trademark of Pioneer
Communications Network, Inc.

ISBN: 0-916217-45-0

Printed in the United States of America

10 9 8 7 6 5 4 3 2 1

5

Forbidden Passions

Chapter One
Innocent Beginnings

The aroma from Nancy's kitchen wafted through the house, luring Bob down the stairs. After church he'd taken off his suit and was now wearing a plaid sport shirt and slacks. Hungry, he cruised into the kitchen and copped a hot biscuit, tossing it in the air to cool it down.

"Bob Hughes," Nancy scolded as if he were still a child instead of a capable doctor, "will you ever learn?" She playfully spanked his hand with her spatula, taking a mother's pride in his clean cut good looks.

Bob grinned, pecked his mother on the cheek, and downed the biscuit greedily. "No one can resist your baking; you know that, Mom."

He admired Nancy's efficiency and calm as she went about the kitchen. She was always neat and calm, no matter what the crisis. Even after having spent hours in the kitchen, not a stray brown hair was out of place and her dress looked starched and as fresh as she did.

Chris Hughes entered and headed straight for the biscuits. Even in his own home, the lawyer's strong presence of authority and command was obvious. Chris was a big-boned man with a strong chin and a generous, even smile.

Bob watched his parents interact, enjoying their closeness. He thought no one could be more distinguished than his father. Recently Chris's thick light hair had grayed to a handsome white, giving him even more of an air of authority.

Chris's smile widened. "Nancy, I never could resist your biscuits," he said, reaching for the baking pan.

"You too . . ." Nancy said, laughing. "No wonder our children behave so."

" 'Cause you've spoiled them all," Chris said, patting his wife's bottom playfully.

"Oh, Chris!" She blushed shooting an embarrassed glance at Bob.

"Not in front of the children," her husband teased. Both men began to chuckle.

"Come on you two," Nancy chided. "Everyone will be here soon and we'll never have enough if you eat it all now."

"Not have enough?" Bob asked, biting into a second biscuit as he surveyed the feast his mother had prepared. "You can feed the world's starving with all this, Mom!"

Nancy smiled. Bob teased her the same way every week. Sunday brunch at the Hughes's household was always a festive affair. He knew his mother thrived on the weekly get-togethers after church. It kept the family close. Mounds of eggs, bacon, biscuits and blueberry muffins, as well as bowls of fresh fruit covered the dining room table this morning. The meal always went smoothly, and Nancy was the master planner.

There was a knock on the kitchen door, but before anyone had time to answer it, Lisa let herself in. "Hi all!" she called. "Guess who's here . . ."

"Oh, hi, Lisa," Bob said unenthusiastically.

"Now is that any way to greet a gal on a beautiful Sunday morning?" Lisa drawled, kissing him boldly on the cheek.

Bob shrugged and took a step away from his former wife. He had to agree she looked wonderful. Lisa was the only redhead he'd ever met who could wear red well. She carried off the crimson dress with flare and style. No one could ever ignore Lisa. She virtually sparkled with personality and fire. He found himself staring at his ex-wife with appreciation. Now, approaching forty, it seemed Lisa improved with age.

Bob shook off the uncomfortable feeling of attraction and asked about their son. "Tom coming?"

"Uh huh." Lisa's green eyes sparkled. "And he's bringing his girl."

Nancy looked up from the pan she was rinsing. "I didn't know Tom was seeing anyone."

"She's an old high school girlfriend," Lisa explained. "He says he's known her for years."

"You haven't met her?" Nancy's tone was disapproving, and Lisa could imagine what the older woman was thinking. *Imagine not meeting your son's date . . . How could you be so lax?*

Lisa changed the subject. "Where's Grandpa Hughes? You know how I love the old lamb."

"In the basement. Tom needed a new bookcase for his office. Grandpa wanted to have it finished for him today."

The doorbell rang and Lisa dashed for the front door.

"That'll be Tom . . . "

"Hi, Mom," Tom said, feeling a bit awkward to encounter Lisa among the Hughes. His mother hadn't been in the family's good graces for quite some time. He stepped through the door and ushered his date in. The girl who lingered shyly behind him was pretty and wholesome, like a model in an Ivory Soap ad.

Bob and Chris were waiting for an introduction, but before Tom could say anything the rest of the family appeared. Tom was glad he had warned Carol about how close his family was. As all the members of the Hughes family converged on her now, he knew she must feel as if she were being judged like a prized Guernsey. Her fair skin flushed as she nervously ran her hand through her short, red hair.

"This is Carol," Tom announced, his deep voice reassuring her. He took Carol's hand, offering her some added support.

She squeezed Tom's hand tightly, taking strength from her tall, sandy-haired escort before working up the nerve to say anything. She was relieved when the words came out right. "Thank you for inviting me."

"I'm so pleased that Tom asked you to join us," Nancy said warmly. "Let's go into the dining room. Brunch is ready and you all must be starving."

Noticing the look of approval on his grandmother's face, Tom breathed a sigh of relief; Carol had passed the first test.

Grateful for Nancy's friendly reception, Carol began to relax. She realized how important it was to make a good impression on Tom's grandmother. He had certainly been specific about that.

As she sat down, Carol looked at Tom with an

expression no one could misinterpret. She was obviously in love with him, and he apparently felt the same way about her.

As the meal progressed, Carol gradually warmed up to Tom's family. The only person she had trouble relating to was his mother, who seemed to make an ostentatious production of everything. By the time brunch was over, Carol was already beginning to feel like a part of the Hughes family.

Nancy was refilling coffee cups when Bob excused himself from the table.

"Bob?" Lisa said with obvious disappointment.

"I have a patient in the Cardiac unit," he explained as he headed for the door.

In a calculated move, Carol insisted on helping Nancy clear the table. She knew she'd receive another set of good marks for her effort.

After the table was cleared, Tom took Carol's hand and led her outside for a stroll by the lake. Chris and Grandpa repaired to the basement, leaving Lisa and Nancy alone.

"Mom, you don't know how much it meant to me to be here today," Lisa said quietly as she stacked the plates.

Even though she was concentrating on the dishes, Nancy couldn't help but be aware of the change in Lisa. "You've been through a rough period, lately," she said. "I sensed that you needed us. You are the mother of my grandson; you'll always be a part of this family."

As Lisa kissed Nancy on the cheek she turned her head away, hoping to hide the tears that stung her eyes.

The corridors of Memorial Hospital were usually

quiet on Sunday morning. Except for the receptionist, who was reading a paperback novel, the lobby was empty. Bob Hughes pushed the elevator button and waited impatiently.

"Bob!"

Turning at the sound of a familiar voice, he found Sean Ryan running toward the elevator. It had been a long time since Bob had seen Sean, and he was shocked at how much the other man had changed. Heavier and with a great deal of gray in his hair, Sean looked distinguished, but much older than Bob remembered him. Sean was panting breathlessly.

"Sean! I heard you'd arrived," Bob exclaimed enthusiastically clasping the other man's hand. He couldn't get over the change in the man. Although they were contemporaries, Bob thought that Sean looked at least ten years older than he did.

"When we left medical school, I never expected we'd be working together again," Sean said, trying to catch his breath.

"We can thank Memorial Hospital for that. The place has been growing rapidly. Now we can afford to add some really impressive men to our staff. I hear that you've made a quite a name for yourself. You're a top surgeon in your field . . . ."

"Don't be modest, Bob. You've made a damn good reputation as a cardiologist too. I've been keeping track, you know. By the way, have you had a chance to meet John Dixon yet? I hear he's joining the staff here too. I always heard he was a good man."

"Tops, I'm told. I'm looking forward to meeting him," Bob agreed.

When the elevator finally arrived the two men

stepped in together. "Hey, I've got a great idea," Sean said. "Why don't you come to dinner tonight and meet my wife?"

"On such short notice?" Bob asked.

"Jennifer won't mind. She loves company. Tonight at six." He thought a moment. "Better make it seven." They reached the third floor and the doors slid open. Sean quickly scribbled his address on the back of a prescription blank. "Wait'll you meet her. You'll love her."

Lisa arrived home feeling warm and happy. She hadn't realized how much she'd missed the family gatherings. There was something special about the Hugheses and she chided herself for being foolish enough to give up Bob. But all hope wasn't lost. Lisa fully intended to try to get Bob back if it was at all humanly possible. The problem was, how?

The past months had been agonizing. Her marriage to Michael Shea had been devastating, and the murder accusation and acquittal of Tom, ghastly. If it weren't for Tom, she didn't know what she would have done.

She smiled at the thought of her son. He had been willing to risk his life and freedom for her. Now that the tensions of the past months had eased, they were finally on good terms with each other once more. Besides, Tom was Bob's son, the only part of her former husband she had left.

Lisa thought of Carol and frowned. Although she seemed to be a nice girl, Lisa resented her for having stolen Tom's affections.

"That's enough!" she chided herself, shaking her red mane proudly and entering her bedroom. When would she ever learn to accept the inevitable? Tom wasn't a boy any longer, and Lisa couldn't hang on to him forever.

The years had been kind to Lisa. She combed her hair back, sprayed it in place and was pleased with the result. After examining the small bottles of perfume on her dresser she picked a light floral scent. Just as she was touching up her makeup, the doorbell rang. Lisa smoothed the hem of the emerald green taffeta dress and opened the door.

She smiled. "Hi, Tod. Right on time." He was always so predictable, she thought. "Come on in."

Tod stood in the doorway, his brown slicked-back hair shining in the light of the streetlamp. "I made reservations at the Steakhouse." He grinned slyly. "It's out by the lake. We'll have a long drive . . ."

A sudden wave of guilt washed over Lisa. Perhaps she should call the whole thing off?

But before she could say anything, Tod swung his arm around her and began to guide her out the door.

Lisa wiggled free. "I'm starved. Let's go," she demanded, marching toward the car.

"Come on in," Sean exclaimed, ushering Bob into his apartment. "Jenny, Bob's here!" he called.

Bob watched a cute brunette emerge from the kitchen. In her casual slacks and pink sweater she seemed totally relaxed. *Just the kind of woman I would have expected Sean to choose*, Bob thought.

Jennifer looked at the room with its upacked boxes scattered throughout the living room and laughed. "You'll have to forgive us. We haven't had much time to unpack yet."

"I'm impressed," Bob said sincerely. "I've never met anyone who could manage to entertain a dinner guest when they're still not settled in."

"That's life," Jennifer said cheerfully. "Can't put it on hold. Besides, people are more important than appearances. Sean's told me so much about you. I just couldn't wait to meet you. Please, have a seat, make yourself comfortable."

"I'm flattered," Bob said, chuckling. "But, where do I sit?"

Jennifer cleared a pile of linens off a chair. "Here. Dinner'll be ready in a minute. In the meantime, why don't you two become reacquainted. I'm sure you have lots to catch up on." With that, she breezed out of the room.

"She's quite a gal, Sean," Bob remarked.

"I thought you'd like her. Really special, isn't she?"

"You're a lucky man."

"Sure am. Wait'll you meet our son, Rick. An up-and-coming surgeon," Sean boasted.

Bob nodded. "My son, Tom, is an attorney now."

"And your wife?"

Bob frowned, hesitating. "I haven't been as lucky as you. Two marriages; both ended in divorce."

"Maybe things will work out better next time," Sean said, seeing that Bob needed some cheering.

"Dinner is served," Jennifer announced as she entered from the kitchen tenuously balancing a large tray. Bob hopped up and lifted the heavy load from her arms. "Where do I put it?"

Jennifer pointed to a box. "On there. We don't have any furniture yet."

The meal was an indoor picnic. Hot, spicy spaghetti,

garlic bread and salad were served on paper plates, and the red wine was poured into plastic bathroom cups decorated with cartoon animals. "I promise, when we get properly settled, we'll treat you to a nice, formal dinner here."

Bob tucked a paper napkin into his collar and dug in. "I doubt that a formal dinner can top this."

After dinner, Sean sifted through one of the boxes and came up with a bottle of brandy. Jennifer took it to the kitchen and returned shortly with liquor-laced coffee and cookies.

Bob took a sip of the coffee and whistled. "Whew, potent."

"I've got to take a snort each day," Sean explained. "Couldn't think of a better way to down it."

Bob looked up at his friend with concern. "Heart?"

Sean nodded. "I should have known I couldn't fool a cardiologist."

"Not that I'm trying to drum up business or anything," Bob quipped. "But why don't you make an appointment so we can keep up with your medical history?"

"I was going to," Sean assured him, "as soon as I had a chance."

"The sooner the better," Jennifer said, a firm warning in her voice. "But enough shop talk, we'll be hearing it every day on the job."

Bob looked up curiously.

"I'm joining the nursing staff at Memorial next week," she announced. "Cardiac care unit."

"Then we'll be working together."

"Seems so."

Bob looked at his watch. "It's getting late. I have to

check in with a patient before I get home." He thanked the Ryans warmly and left.

As Bob drove back to the hospital it began to rain. The drops were soon pelting the car so persistently that he had a hard time seeing where he was going.

The cardiac care unit, Jennifer had said. For some reason, her words had pleased Bob tremendously.

Chapter Two

The Girl in the Red Convertible

Bob turned to watch Jennifer stroll down the corridor. He smiled, and she warmly returned his greeting. Ever since his two marriages had ended so badly, Bob had felt at odds with most women. But Jennifer seemed different. Perhaps the fact that she was married to Sean made it easier for Bob to feel comfortable about her. Yet, in the depths of his heart, he knew it was more than that. He found her whole personality appealing. Her relaxed and natural ways made him feel more alive and vital than he'd felt in months.

"How's the job treating you?" he asked as she approached.

"Memorial's a fine hospital, Bob. I'm really pleased to be on staff. Sean said it was tops. He was right, of course."

Bob became serious. "Speaking of your husband. He hasn't made an appointment to see me yet."

Jennifer frowned. "I suspected as much. Denial is his way of handling the problem."

Hoping for privacy, Bob led her to the corner of the

hall. "But he should know better," he murmured.

"Frankly, Bob," Jennifer said with a toss of her head. "I can't think of any worse patient than a doctor. I dread having to treat one."

Bob laughed. "I suppose you're right. We are notoriously lax about ourselves."

"It's that know-it-all attitude you doctors have," Jennifer quipped. "You believe you're omnipotent and invulnerable. It's just one of your less admirable and predictable professional traits."

Bob laughed. "Come on. We're not *all* that bad."

Jennifer's cheerful facade began to crumble. "Bob, I'm really worried about Sean. He doesn't look well, and I know he's having trouble breathing. The angina is worse, too. He tries to hide it, but I see how often he's taking his nitroglycerin. It's much too frequent."

"I'll try to coax him into an exam today," Bob promised taking her hand. "I'll tie him down if I have to."

"Thanks, Bob. I don't know what I'd do if something happened to him. We've been together so long . . . and I love him so much."

Bob was impressed with her devotion and felt somewhat cheated by his lack of someone of his own to cherish. "You married right after med school, didn't you?".

"Yes. But we were high school sweethearts. In fact, we grew up together. Sean felt it best we wait to marry until he finished most of the course work. It was a wise decision. It gave me a chance to finish nursing school also." Jennifer looked stricken. "I've never been without him, Bob. My life would be empty without Sean."

"Jennifer," Bob said, enjoying the sound of her name

on his lips, "I'll do my best with him. I promise."

The phone rang and Jennifer picked it up. "Nurses's station, cardiac care," she said with efficiency. She waved a goodbye and smiled as Bob took his patients' charts and entered the unit.

The phone rang loudly, awakening Bob from a deep sleep. He turned on the light and glanced at the clock. "Four AM. Why doesn't anyone ever get sick in the daytime?"

He picked up the receiver before it could ring again and awaken the entire household. "Bob Hughes," he said sleepily.

"Doctor, it's Alice in the C.C.U. I hate to wake you, but Mr. Avery's gone sour."

Instantly alert, Bob gave the nurse some quick orders and dressed hurriedly. He was out of the house in less than five minutes.

The rain had worsened, and it had begun to freeze. He went through a stoplight and a police car followed him for a short distance. He saw it turn off when it got close enough to see his medical plates and that he was heading toward Memorial. He was soaked by the time he got into the hospital, and shivered as he stripped off his coat in the elevator.

"Doctor Hughes!" Alice ran out of the cardiac care unit as if she were afire.

"Avery?" Bob asked, thinking the worst.

"We've tried everything," Alice said desperately. "He's still hanging on, but barely."

When Alice reported the patient's responses, Bob didn't understand why his reactions were so odd. "You're sure you followed my orders?"

"Yes, doctor, but!"

"But what?" Bob demanded as he strode to Mr. Avery's bedside. Another doctor, a stranger with a haystack of golden hair, was leaning over his patient.

"Not good," the doctor said when Bob entered. He turned, and seeing Bob, offered his hand. "John Dixon."

Bob shook John's hand and looked at his patient. After a quick exam, he consulted with Dixon. "I can't understand why his blood pressure is so depressed." He lifted Avery's eyelid. "And his responses are much too sluggish."

"He was fibrillating. We used the paddles," John reported. "Then I administered a lidocayne I.V."

"You did what?" Bob shouted. He rarely raised his voice; now the nurses were astonished. "Didn't you read his chart?"

"There was no time."

"I prescribed Bretylol. If you'd taken the trouble to familiarize yourself with the patient before jumping in, you'd have learned he's allergic to lidocayne. No wonder there's such a deep depression of the nervous system."

"In emergency situations, lidocayne is the medication most often recommended, " John reminded him.

"Usually, yes," Bob agreed. "But not in this case. We're lucky he didn't go into a coma or die."

Bob could see that John Dixon was not a man to back down. In actuality, he was right, lidocayne was more frequently used, but this wasn't the emergency room and there was a chart on the patient available.

Bob prescribed a stimulant.

"It's already been administered," Alice informed him.

"Doctor Dixon prescribed one."

Slightly mollified, Bob took John by the arm and led him out into the hallway. "At least you remedied the situation. Next time read the chart!" He almost said, *Stay away from my patients,* but decided, that just maybe, his negative reaction to the new staff doctor had been too hasty.

The storm had ended and it had become a sparkling fall Monday morning. Tom Hughes had gotten up at six o'clock, taken a run around the block, showered, and was off to the law offices of Lowell and Hughes. He frequently went to work early and came home late. The fact that his grandfather was a founder of the firm only made his performance more open to scrutiny. He was bound and determined to be a good lawyer and become a partner someday.

Tom was dedicated, skilled, and proud of his family's firm. Grandfather Hughes had always been a role model he'd emulated, and his dad's success as a doctor had always given him a sense of pride. At six feet, he stood taller than his father, and he towered over his petite mother. No one approved of his full beard, but it was the one concession to individualism he allowed himself in the conservative legal world in which he worked.

He knew the Hughes family was proud of him and he felt closest to Grandma Hughes, who'd always been a mainstay in his life and had brought him up when Lisa had deserted him as an infant. Tom had never resented his mother's neglect. Nancy had provided all of the security and love any child would ever need. And with Bob's love and Chris's stability, no child could ever have had a better home.

He had been very young when Lisa and Bob divorced, and Tom knew a baby had to have been an inhibiting factor to a lone struggling woman. Not that Lisa had struggled for very long. Tom gave his mother credit for possessing a talent for improving her lot in life. Lisa never remained single for very long and seemed to have a knack for attracting the wealthy men of the world. He knew it was fruitless to resent his mother and was doing his best to keep their relationship workable. In fact, lately, he was pleased to think of Lisa as a friend as well as his mother.

Tom cruised up to the stoplight. A car horn honked and he turned toward the sound. To his left, in a brand new, red Mustang convertible, was the most stunning girl he'd ever seen. She had the convertible top down, in spite of the cool morning. She waved at him.

Tom smiled and waved back.

She signaled for him to roll the window down. The light changed and the car behind him honked, forcing him to get going. Tom drove to the next light slowly, keeping pace with the convertible. He prayed for a red light at the next corner. It cooperated, and he rolled down the window.

"Hi." Her green eyes sparkled and her voice sang.

He turned down the radio. "Hi!" He called back, but before he could say anymore the light changed. He paced the convertible once again. The girl winked, then turned left.

With no intention of permitting that beautiful creature to get out of his sight, Tom cut his car across traffic to follow her, causing a blaring of horns.

The red car pulled off to the curb and Tom parked

behind it. He got out of the car quickly and walked over to the Mustang.

"Hi, I'm Tom Hughes."

She patted the seat next to hers, inviting him into the car. "Meredith Halliday. I just arrived in town."

"To my good fortune," Tom responded, utterly entranced.

"How about some breakfast?" she suggested.

He was tempted, but a glance at his watch told him it was already eight o'clock. "Can't. Gotta go to work," he said with more than a touch of regret.

"Too bad. I hate to eat alone."

Realizing that if he let her go now he would probably never see this alluring woman again, Tom blurted out, "How about dinner, then?"

"Okay. Seven thirty. I'm staying at the Oakdale Inn." She revved up the car and was gone.

Tom felt as if he'd been hit by a brick. He got back into his car and went to the office, but even before he got there he knew he wouldn't be able to concentrate on the law that day. Never had a day moved so slowly. He couldn't wait to see Meredith again.

Bob was on the ward when he heard his name called. "Doctor Hughes, to the emergency room. Stat."

Bob told the nurse on the floor to call E.R. to tell them he was on his way, then he hurried to the elevator, saw that both cars were as far as they could get from where he was, and took the stairs instead. He'd been dashing up and down the stairs at Memorial for so many years, he was sure that's what kept him in such good physical shape. His odd hours had never allowed time for a regular exercise regime. He beat the elevator down and rushed into the emergency room.

Jennifer, tears staining her pale face, ran toward him. "It's Sean!"

He spoke on the run. "I'll let you know how he is as soon as I can."

By the time Bob arrived, Sean's I.V. wasn't dripping, and the monitor showed flat. Bob leaned over Sean, pumping on his chest to stimulate his heart to beat again. He injected adrenalin into the heart, tried the paddles and when they didn't do it, pumped again.

"Nothing, Doctor," the nurse wathing the monitor said.

"Sean. It's Bob. Sean!"

"Give up, Doctor, it's been too long." The nurse's voice came through a haze of grief. He knew he couldn't help his friend anymore.

Bob wiped the perspiration off his face, splashed it with water, waited a moment to gather his courage, and went out to Jennifer.

She ran up to him with both hope and dread in her eyes.

"He's gone," Bob said softly. "There was nothing I could do."

Jennifer didn't say anything, didn't move at all. It was as if she had been turned to stone. Bob recognized the signs. Shock was not an unusual reaction to a great loss. He was feeling some himself. He took Jennifer gently into his arms to comfort her, and together they shared their grief.

Tom put a little more effort than usual into dressing. He tried on most of the clothes in his closet and found them lacking. Finally, he chose a blue blazer with brass buttons, gray slacks, and a white shirt with a red tie close to the color of her car. He picked up his raincoat and headed for the hotel.

Meredith was waiting in the lobby. There was no missing her in her bright red coat. It set off her luxurious dark hair with fiery highlights, and her red lips smiled invitingly.

When he saw her, Tom felt as if he were being drawn into a fire. Oddly, he didn't mind the possiblity of getting burned.

"I'm famished. Haven't eaten since breakfast," she told him before he even had a chance to say hello.

Tom smiled weakly. He had no appetite left at all— except for Meredith.

They had dinner at a restaurant he couldn't afford, and Meredith ordered the most expensive appetizer on the menu, a chef's salad for two, and lobster.

Tom didn't care what he ate. He couldn't take his eyes off her. He simply sat there thinking what it would be like to be alone with her.

When the check came Tom was astonished and more than a little embarrassed. He shuffled through his wallet and bit his lip. "I don't seem to have enough cash," he said lamely.

"No problem," Meredith told him. She pulled a huge wad of bills out of her purse. "This enough?"

Tom took what he needed and returned the rest. "You shouldn't be carrying so much money around. It's not safe."

"Are you telling me that your little metropolis of Oakdale is dangerous?" she asked.

"That's not what I meant."

She laughed. "I know. But I always carry a lot of

money. I like the color."

They had driven to the restaurant in Meredith's car. She stood up, handed Tom the keys, and smiled. "How about a nightcap in my room at the hotel?"

Everyone in Oakdale knew the Hughes family and, although completely overcome by her, he didn't want to cause a scandal. Tom thought twice about Meredith's invitation.

"You afraid of what people will think?" she asked, seeing Tom's hesitation.

"Yes. My granddad's quite a respected lawyer and my father's a doctor. A lot of people in town know who I am."

"Then use the back stairs. No one ever uses stairs in a hotel."

"You know you're right." He grinned.

For Tom, in his eagerness to be alone with this marvelous creature, every stop light in town seemed to be conspiring against him. He counted at least five red lights in the short stretch between the restaurant and hotel. He thought they would never get back to the hotel. At the next light, Tom glanced at his companion. The wet street was reflecting the lights in crazy patterns, and Meredith's hair had picked up the colors also. She looked unreal. He could hardly believe he was with this tantalizing creature.

The tap on his shoulder brought Tom back to his driving. "Light's changed," Meredith reminded him.

"Oh, sure," he said as he stepped on the gas.

"Room 812," Meredith whispered to him when they reached the hotel and had parked the car.

"Eight floors?"

"You're the one who's worried about appearances,"

she said, and walked toward the elevator.

Minutes later, Tom arrived at Meredith's door. "Whew! After that hike up here, I need a drink," he said, breathing heavily. He was carrying his coat and had opened his jacket.

Meredith poured some red wine over ice. "Here, this'll help."

Tom drank the wine. Instead of cooling him, he felt warmer than ever. Meredith's presence was as intoxicating as the wine and he was finding it hard to contain himself.

"Mind if I take off my tie?" he said, loosening it.

"Mind?" she asked. "Let me help?"

As she reached to loosen his tie, Meredith's hands felt cool against his throat. Tom gulped in an effort to maintain control as the tie slipped off. Meredith draped it over her shoulder and performed a little twist using the tie as a prop. She ran it softly over his face.

"God, you're beautiful," Tom said as he followed her around the room. Her graceful movements tantalized, drawing him closer and closer.

"You're not so bad yourself," she said, fluttering the tie invitingly. "Tom Hughes. I like the sound of it."

"Where'd you come from?" he asked, fully expecting her to say Olympus.

"Oh, from here and there. I'm a vagabond runaway. Evil guardian and all of that."

"I'm Sir Galahad, then, your knight to the rescue."

"I might call upon you for that someday," she said, drawing close to him and taking the empty glass from his hand.

Tom breathed heavily as she touched him. Her perfume was exotic and heady. He reached for her and she quickly ducked away.

"I won't be able to stand much more of this," he panted.

"Neither will I," she said seductively. Meredith went for the buttons on his shirt. Her touch made him even warmer and he stripped off the shirt. She turned so he could reach the zipper on her dress. He slowly pulled it down and saw the wonder of her bare back. His eyes widened and his pulse raced.

Fleetingly, he thought of Carol and her wholesome prettiness, but all thought of her disappeared when Meredith, her bronze skin glowing, stood invitingly before him.

He stroked her hair, then ran his hand down the smooth flesh of her back. She smelled of flowers, and the cold fall night was warmed by her presence.

The day was dismal, just right for a funeral. A cold drizzle had dampened the grass, and there was a forecast of snow. Jennifer's face was pale, her eyes reddened by tears. Accompanied by her son, Rick, whose protective arm about her shoulder kept the hostile world at bay, Jennifer slowly left her husband's grave.

Bob walked over to join them. "If there's anything I can do . . ."

"Everything's taken care of, Dr. Hughes. But thanks anyway." Rick helped his mother into the limousine, then spoke to Bob alone.

Bob could see Jennifer in her son. He was darker, favoring his father's coloring, but his fine features and the mouth were Jennifer's. "There is one thing, Dr. Hughes. I don't think she should be alone right now. Do you think its possible for me to join the staff at Memorial?" Rick suggested.

"Send me your credentials. I'll see what I can do."

Rick got into the limousine beside his grieving mother.

Jennifer leaned out the window as they drove off. "Call me, Bob, please."

Tom was beside himself with excitement. "Mom, wait'll you meet her. I just know you'll love Meredith."

Lisa had never seen Tom in this way. She wondered what the girl would really be like and what was Tom doing about Carol?

There was a knock on the door. "That's her now," Tom said, dashing to open it.

God! Lisa thought. *He's really smitten with this girl.*

Lisa's first impression of Meredith was anything but positive. Although the girl's clothes were obviously expensive, Lisa thought they were garish.

"Mrs. Shea," Meredith said, as she offered her hand. "Tom's told me all about you."

Lisa stood back appraising the girl. "Oh, really?"

"He says we have a lot in common."

"Oh, he does, does he?" Lisa threw Tom a dirty look. Did he think she was that brassy?

"We're going to the Steakhouse," Tom said. "Want to join us, Mom?"

"I don't think so," Lisa answered. "I think I'll settle down in front of a big fire with a book."

Meredith smiled, and Lisa knew the girl was pleased not to have her in their company.

Hours later, Lisa impatiently waited up for Tom to return. She'd hardly ever interfered with her son's social life, but something about Meredith was disturbing. Maybe she saw something of herself in the girl. That alone was a scary thought. She put it out of her mind. She'd made great strides in changing and was proud of her accomplishment.

It was very late by the time Tom got home, but Lisa was still awake and ready to confront him with her reservations about Meredith.

"But, Mom, you only met her for a few minutes, give her a chance," Tom said after his mother had voiced her concern.

"What about Carol? Have you seen anything of her lately?"

"I'll call her next week, Mom. I promise," he answered sheepishly.

"Meredith is not good for you, Tom. Take my advice and stay away from her. I'm sure your father would tell you the same thing."

"It's nobody's concern but mine," Tom snapped. "Don't interfere in my life."

"But Tom . . ."

"It's late, I'm going to bed." Tom stalked out of the room, cutting Lisa off.

Lisa had been calling Bob incessantly, and he hadn't called back yet. She knew he was probably trying to avoid her, but she was determined to see him about Tom and his new girlfriend. Finally, in frustration, she headed for Memorial Hosptial. She was told Bob was up in C.C.U. and headed for the fifth floor. Through the glass window, she could see her former husband and a nurse busy with a patient.

"Can I help you?" the duty nurse asked.

"I'm waiting for Doctor Hughes."

"He's busy."

"I can see that," Lisa said impatiently. "I'll wait for him."

"We really don't encourage visitors here."

"I'm not a visitor," Lisa snapped. "I'll wait."

Lisa watched Bob and the nurse working together. She saw the smile that passed between them and felt a tinge of jealousy which she tried to suppress. "Nonsense, you can't be jealous of every nurse he works with," she told herself. "That's crazy."

Bob and the attractive nurse came out of the treatment room laughing. "Bob," the nurse said. "You can charm the birds out of the trees."

Angry at the woman's familiarity with Bob, Lisa walked over and deliberately placed herself between them. "Bob," she said. "I must talk to you about Tom."

Obviously disturbed by her appearance at the hospital, he scowled. "Not here, Lisa."

"But I've been leaving messages for you and you never get back to me. It's important, really important."

"I'm sorry," he said, realizing the women had never met. "Jennifer Ryan, this is Lisa Shea."

Lisa had heard of the death of Bob's old friend, Sean, and knew this must be his widow. She never knew quite what to say in such situations. "I'm sorry about your husband," she finally managed to murmur.

"Bob's been a great help," Jennifer said. "I don't know what I would have done without him. He's even arranged for my son to join the staff here."

"How nice," Lisa snapped. "Bob has always been generous that way."

Bob knew Lisa well enough to see through the

sweetness. "I'll call you tonight, Lisa," he said firmly.

"Just make sure you do," Lisa said as she left.

"She seemed very upset," Jennifer commented.

"That's Lisa, Jen. Always making mountains out of molehills. She'll calm down. She always does."

Jennifer went back to work and Bob, watching her, couldn't help but compare her with Lisa. They were as opposite as any two women could be, and he was glad he could be there for Jen when she needed him most. He'd even introduced her to his Mom and Dad and they were as taken with her as he was. But then, why shouldn't they be? He had known there was something special about her the moment they'd met.

Fate had drawn them together; now he was beginning to think he wanted the arrangement to be permanent.

Chapter Three

One Brother or Another

Meredith aimed the snowball at Tom's back-side. After it hit, he picked up a handful of snow and smashed it into her head. She tossed her dark, shining cascade of hair and laughed.

"I'll get you for that, Tom Hughes!"

"Yeah, when?" Tom said, putting his arms around her tightly.

"How about right now," she said, kissing him hard on the mouth. When their lips parted she beckoned him to follow her to the lodge.

Tom knew it was insane to have come with Meredith to the exclusive Lodge on the Lake, but then he hadn't had a sane day since he'd met her. He certainly couldn't afford the luxurious place. However Meredith seemed to be able to take care of the finances, and he'd long since given up worrying about appearances.

He found her intoxicating. She certainly had proven habit forming, he thought as they mounted the stairs. She had bewitched him, and he was enjoying the spell. A fire crackled invitingly in their room and Meredith had arranged for a crock of hot spiced cider to be delivered. She laced it with rum and handed him a steaming mug. Then she turned off the lights and they sat quietly in the flickering firelight.

"I could stay like this forever," Tom murmured. Meredith was wearing a red angora sweater that felt sensuous to his touch. He nuzzled her neck and she nipped his shoulder.

"Ouch!" he exclaimed.

"Couldn't help it, you bring out the wildcat in me."

"And you bring out the animal in me," he said, shoving her down onto the sheepskin rug in front of the fireplace. They tossed playfully for a moment, before Tom pinned Meredith to the floor and covered her mouth with his. Tom's flesh burned as he reached under the soft sweater to touch her even softer flesh. His emotions exploded, and his heart pounded. They spent the rest of the night snuggled in the comfort of each other's arms.

"I simply didn't know who to turn to," the distraught Lisa said to the assembled Hughes clan. Her favorite person, Grandpa Hughes, gave her a smile of encouragement. Donald sat on the couch next to his father and Nancy had just come in from the kitchen. "I can't get anywhere with him," Lisa said. "Now he's off somewhere with that girl, and I'm really worried."

Nancy handed Lisa a cup of coffee and a fresh apple tart. "I understand, dear. What did Bob say?"

"That's the problem, Mom. Bob is either too busy at Memorial or off somewhere. I never connect with him. It's almost as if he were purposely avoiding me."

Nancy slowly nodded her head. "Possibly, you didn't

make the problem quite clear enough to him," Chris said as if he were preparing a case for court.

"God knows I've tried. Tom's gotten an apartment I know he can't afford. He's out every night, and I know he must be running out of money. I can't imagine how he's paying for all those restaurants and things."

"He's been late to the office lately, too," Chris added, "and his work is certainly not up to par. I agree with you, Lisa. Something's going on."

Lisa cheered some. She hardly ever got Dad Hughes to agree with anything she said, but this time both he and Mom Hughes were on her side. She couldn't help but wonder if Tom's problem may actually prove to be a help to her. His parents' support might even make Bob take notice of her again.

"Maybe I should talk to Bob for you," Donald suggested. "It's about time he and I got together anyway."

Lisa looked to Donald with gratitude. "You'd do that for me?"

"Sure," he said warmly. "Tom's my nephew, after all."

Donald met Bob in the Hospital Cafeteria for lunch the next day. "You eat this stuff all the time?" he asked his brother while examining a rather limp ham sandwich.

"You get used to it," Bob said stoically.

"Maybe *you* do," Donald said, putting the sandwich back on his plate and staring at it with distaste.

"You said you had something important to talk about. I'm sure it has nothing to do with hospital food."

"Lisa—"

"Lisa! Again!" Bob interrupted.

"She's concerned about Tom, and this time we all agree with her."

Bob raised an eyebrow. "All?"

"Mom and Dad are worried about him too. Where have you been these past few weeks? Lisa says she's been trying to reach you for days," Donald explained.

"I've been busy."

"Doctoring?" Don asked, knowing there was more.

"That and other things."

"Would those other things be named Jennifer?"

Bob grinned and nodded.

"You know if you hadn't seen her first, I might have made a play for that lady. She's something special."

"I know," Bob said. "Now what's this about Tom?"

"He's met this girl, Meredith Halliday, and he's gone off the deep end. He's spending money like water, and Dad's concerned about his work at the office."

"He's a grown man," Bob said. "I don't think there's much we can say."

"Come on, Bob, you're his father!"

"I know that! I just believe in permitting one's children to make their own mistakes once in a while."

"Even when they might wreck their entire future?"

"It can't be that bad."

"You really have your head in the sand, Bob. Talk to Tom. See for yourself."

Bob looked at his watch. "I've gotta go, but you've convinced me. As soon as I find the time, I'll talk to him."

"Lisa'll be relieved," Donald said as he got up to leave. "Make it soon, Bob, and after you talk to Tom, give Lisa a call. Please."

"Sure," Bob said as he walked to the other side of the cafeteria, where Jennifer sat.

A few moments later Don saw them leave together.

* * *

"Carol?" Nancy pushed her grocery cart toward the girl.

Carol put a box of cornflakes into her cart and looked up to see Nancy. "Mrs. Hughes, how nice to run into you. How have you been?" she asked.

The girl seemed self-conscious and uncomfortable. "Is something the matter, dear?" Nancy probed.

"It's nothing. I'm fine, really."

No matter what Carol said, it was obvious to Nancy that the girl was upset. She had liked Carol from the very first moment they'd met and wanted to help the girl. "Let's talk," she suggested. "Why don't you come home with me for a cup of tea?"

"I wouldn't want to inconvenience you."

"Nonsense, dear. I'd love some company. All the menfolk are off doing heaven knows what and I'm all alone in the house."

"In that case, I'd love to come," Carol said. She pushed her cart to the checkout counter and followed Nancy Hughes home.

Nancy served a slice of homemade fruitcake with the tea and then broached the problem again. "What is it, dear. You seem so unhappy."

"I am," Carol said after a moment's hesitation. "I just don't understand . . ." She stopped speaking, doing her best to hold back the tears.

"What don't you understand, child?" Nancy asked gently.

"Tom. I love him so, and I haven't seen him for weeks."

Nancy sat upright and frowned. "Tom! I might have guessed."

"He doesn't call anymore. No, that's not right. He called once and asked me how I was. Like I was some stranger. He hasn't called since. Is he all right?"

"He's in good health," Nancy responded, skirting the question.

"That's not what I meant," Carol said, breaking into tears. "He's seeing someone else. I saw him with a girl at the movies the other night. She's beautiful, and she dresses so well. I know I'm no match for her, Mrs. Hughes."

"He's infatuated with her," Nancy explained. "Girls like that seem to be able to bewitch a man, but that type of girl can't hold a man long. They have no substance."

"I wish I could believe that," Carol said, using a napkin to dry her eyes. "But I can't."

Nancy put a sympathetic arm about Carol's shoulders. "Crying helps," she said, "Just let it all out, dear."

Donald walked down the frozen drive, wondering why he was dating Sylvia at all. It's not that they didn't enjoy each other's company, but something was missing. Sparks just didn't fly when he was with her. He thought of Bob and Jennifer, and couldn't avoid a twinge of jealousy. Jennifer was a very attractive woman, one who would make any man sit up and take notice.

He got into his car and drove to Tom's new apartment. It was in a new luxury building, one of many that had been built recently to accommodate Oakdale's growth. The old town was changing, losing some of its small-town flavor. It was a mixed blessing, Donald mused. Good for business, but changing a good way of life.

Donald had decided to drop in without warning. The doorman let him in. "Mr. Hughes?" Donald asked.

"Apartment 6M, sir. Shall I buzz him?"

"No. I want to surprise him." As he was waiting for the elevator Donald looked around the lobby. It was furnished extravagantly. Nouveau riche bad taste, Don decided. How the hell could Tom afford to live here? He wondered.

Rock music was blaring from Tom's apartment. Donald rang the bell three times and knocked loudly. The door opened.

"Hi!" Meredith said, opening the door.

"Tom here?"

"Sure is. In the bedroom," she said, tossing her head in that general direction. She was wearing a fine turquoise silk robe, with ecru lace trim. The robe slipped open revealing a smooth rounded white breast, and Donald got a hint of what Tom saw in her.

"Who should I tell him is calling?" she asked, running her hand through her luxurious dark hair. Donald almost laughed aloud, but controlled the urge. He couldn't help thinking there was a hint of Scarlett O'Hara in the girl.

Tom, wearing a rich green silk robe with black velvet lapels, came out of the bedroom. "Merry? Where'd you disappear to?"

"She's right here," Donald answered.

Tom stopped in his tracks. He finally managed a rather choked, "Uncle Don, what are you doing here?"

"Can we talk?" Donald asked.

"Now?"

"No better time." He turned to Meredith. "Don't you

have someplace you can go, young lady?"

Tom nodded to Meredith and she disappeared into the bedroom. It was mostly white with touches of browns and reds. All the furnishings were ultra modern, and everything looked new and costly. He put his hands to his ears to block out the music. "Can you turn that thing down, please."

Tom shut the music off completely.

Donald whistled. "Some setup you have here. I wish I could afford it. How do you manage it?"

"I manage," Tom said evasively.

"I can see that. She paying?"

"That's none of your business."

Don shook his head. "She's paying. Well, that explains some of it. What the hell do you think you're doing, Tom?"

"I know exactly what I'm doing and it's none of your business."

"That's where you're wrong, young man. Your family's very concerned about you. Your mother is beside herself with worry. Can't you see you've completely lost perspective. Who is this girl anyway?"

"She's new in town."

"Is that all you know about her?"

"What's there to know? I like her. That's all that's important."

"Yeah," Donald recalled his earlier glimpse of Meredith's charms. "Well, I can understand your attraction to her. She's beautiful. But don't you think it's gone a bit too far? I never expected to have a gigolo in the family!"

"It's not that way at all. She's just helping out with the rent."

"With most of it," Donald said matter of factly. There's no way you can possibly afford all of this on what you're paid at Lowell and Hughes. I bet that robe you're wearing would cost a week's salary in itself."

"Merry is used to having the finer things," Tom said in defense.

"You included?" Don asked.

"Why not? We love each other."

"I think you have love confused with lust, Tom. They're not the same at all. She's not the kind of girl—"

"I intend to marry Meredith, Uncle Donald. Don't say anything you'll regret."

"Marry her! You don't mean it!"

"I'm completely serious. So now you can go back and tell the family I have no intention of giving her up, no matter what they think. And I'd appreciate it if you'd all mind your own business." Tom pointed to the door.

Feeling completely defeated, Donald left. He didn't know how he was going to break the news to the family.

The next evening, Lisa waited impatiently for Donald to tell what had happened when he spoke to Tom. "Well, did he listen to you?" she demanded.

"Not exactly," Don said.

"Then what?"

"You were right, Lisa. The girl is bad news. He's living in a style he certainly can't afford, and she's encouraging it. In fact, she's paying for a good deal of it."

"She's paying!" Nancy exclaimed. "Oh, my."

"It's worse than we thought, then," Chris said, leaning back in his leather chair.

Don nodded. "Much worse. She's really got her hooks into him."

"What should we do?" Lisa asked.

"He certainly wouldn't listen to me. Says he intends to marry her."

"Marry her! My God, Donald. That would be a disaster. We don't know anything about the girl. Did he tell you anything at all?"

"Not a thing. She's wealthy and spoiled. That was easy to see. From what I saw, I think she's always been able to get anything she's ever wanted. And she most definitely wants Tom."

They were all aghast at the news. Lisa was agitated to the point of tears. "Oh, Donald, what shall we do now?" she moaned.

"Bob said he'd speak to Tom. Maybe he'll be able to talk some sense into him. But I wouldn't be too optimistic about it. Tom can be damned stubborn."

Bob and Lisa met at his office in the hospital. It was a beautifully decorated room, with a dark green rug and a soft black leather couch, which he slept on when he couldn't leave the hospital. The desk was a rich mahogany, polished until it shone. Not a book was out of place, yet it was obviously a room he spent a great deal of time in.

"I'm sorry I didn't talk to Tom sooner," Bob said frankly. "Until Don told me about the problem I hadn't realized how bad it was."

"I don't know why you wouldn't listen to me. I tried to tell you."

"I know. Tom wouldn't pay any attention to me either."

"Did you meet her?" Lisa said, bristling at the thought of Meredith.

"Briefly. She's very attractive."

"If you like the type. I didn't think that kind appealed to you."

Bob laughed. "I said she's attractive, not desirable, Lisa. Besides, she's a little young for me, don't you think?"

"I certainly do," Lisa said with determination. She blinked her eyes and fussed with the ruffle on her blouse. "Especially when there's a lot of other women," she said seductively.

"You know, Lisa, you've still got all that fire in you that I loved so much."

"Wanna try some cooking," she teased.

"Some other time, maybe."

Those were the most encouraging words Bob had said to her in months. Lisa smiled. "A rain check then."

"Bob?"

The door opened and Jennifer peeked in. She saw Lisa, then hesitated. "I'm sorry, I'll come back later."

"It's all right, Jenny. Lisa's just going."

"Oh, yes," Lisa said, picking up her purse. "I've got to run. I'm managing the Wade Bookstore, you know."

"I've been meaning to get some reading in," Jennifer said sweetly. "Maybe we'll run into each other again."

"Maybe," Lisa said, hustling out the door. "Bye now, Bob."

"Problems?" Jennifer asked after Lisa had left.

"Tom. He's involved with a girl. But forget about that. What's up?"

"I'm going to have to beg off tonight. Something's come up."

"Oh?"

"I have to spend some time with Rick. He seems

depressed," Jennifer explained.

"That's understandable. He lost his father not too long ago."

"I don't think it's that. He seems to get agitated every time I leave the house with you. I think he thinks I'm seeing too much of you, Bob."

"Never too much," Bob quipped, but he looked worried.

"To be honest, I'm worried about Rick. Maybe I'll be able to draw him out and find out what's bothering him."

"Both of us have sons with problems. I always said we had a lot in common."

Jennifer smiled weakly. "You don't mind waiting awhile, do you?" she asked.

"Of course not. I've been running around like a madman lately. I could use a long night's sleep. You're quite a distraction, you know."

She laughed. "I know. I've been pretty busy too. But I love being with you. You've been such a help. I couldn't have survived Sean's death without you. I'll never know how to thank you."

Bob came over to her and kissed her lightly on the cheek. "You already have, Jenny."

The Wade Bookstore had been founded by Penny Hughes and her husband Neil Wade, before he died. Because Penny couldn't stand to live with the sad memories Oakdale held for her, she'd gone to England. Lisa had taken over management of the store just recently, after the last manager quit. Although she had a good deal of money, she still needed something to occupy her time. The bookstore was always full of interesting people and she was seldom alone. It was perfect for her. She had worked hard to put the store into order and now it was a cozy place, full of antique books as well as the latest releases. It smelled a little dusty, but Lisa thought that added charm.

She put her hand to her chin and looked at the neat stacks.

You know, I've never read any of these. But I'll just bet Jennifer has, she thought. *I only wish I had had the incentive to learn all this stuff when I was a girl.* "Well, Lisa, it's never too late!" she said with determination, picking a volume of Shakespeare off the shelf.

She had just reached the end of *Romeo and Juliet* when Donald came in. "Hi, Lisa." He saw tears in her eyes. "What's wrong?"

She showed him the open book. "It's so sad."

"*Romeo and Juliet?* I didn't know you liked Shakespeare."

"There are lots of things you don't know about me, Donald Hughes. Of course I like Shakespeare. I *love* Shakespeare."

"What do you think of *The Taming of the Shrew?*"

"Why, Donald Hughes, that's Bob's line!" She thought it wise to go on to another topic before he found out just how ignorant she was. "What are you doing here anyway?"

"Any luck with Tom?"

"No," she said anxiously. "Bob didn't get anywhere with him, either. There's just got to be something we can do."

"Well hello, Lisa. Donald."

Lisa looked up to see Jennifer, still in her nurse's whites, standing at the counter. "Hello, Jennifer. You really did hurry over."

"What do you have in the way of mysteries?" Jennifer asked, while browsing through the magazines on the rack near the door.

"They're in that row over there, behind the science fiction."

"You haven't been by the house with Bob lately," Donald said.

Jennifer seemed distracted and hesitated. "It's been a grind at Memorial. I'm just bushed. I decided maybe I needed a break."

Jennifer seemed overly nervous. The excuse didn't ring true to Lisa and she cocked her head with interest. Could something be wrong between Jennifer and Bob, she wondered.

Bob dropped in on Jennifer late that evening, after he'd finished at Memorial. She'd just washed her hair and had it wrapped in a towel. She was wearing a blue terry robe and fuzzy pink slippers, and she looked something like a little girl getting ready for bed. She smelled of soap and talc and was irresistible. He put his arm around her waist and sniffed.

"You smell great."

"Mom, who was at the door?" Rick stopped in his tracks when he saw Bob. "Isn't it kind of late to drop in?" he demanded coldly.

"I saw the light and knew you were up." He thought about what he'd just said. *Why am I making excuses to him?* He ignored Rick. "How about a hot cup of something, Jenny. It's freezing out there and I'm numb to the bone."

"Hot chocolate?"

"Great."

"Want to share a cup of cocoa with us, Rick?"

"No thanks, Mom." He glowered at Bob and went back to his bedroom.

Bob followed Jennifer into the kitchen and watched as she heated water for the chocolate. "I'm afraid you're not very popular with my son these days," Jennifer said apologetically.

"Is that why you've been avoiding me?"

"I thought he'd calm down after a while. Maybe he needs more time to adjust to Sean's death. But he seems to be all the more possessive of me each day."

"Therapy?" Bob suggested.

"I don't think it's a serious problem. We both feel the loss. He'll get over it soon."

"I don't know," Bob said. "He seemed awfully belligerent. He's been giving me some problems at Memorial also."

"Why didn't you say something?"

"It's being handled by the Chief of Staff. Nothing to get excited about. Maybe I should have a talk with him myself."

"No!" Jennifer nearly shouted. "Please, Bob, leave him alone."

They drank the cocoa in silence. "That's better," Bob said. "I think I can brave the cold again now."

"Must you leave so soon?" Jennifer asked.

Bob indicated the other room. "I think it's best. Don't you?"

"I suppose so, but I do miss being with you."

"Not half as much as I do."

Bob took her in his arms and kissed her. She smelled like a fresh summer day, and he wanted to stay, to keep her in his arms through the night. "Oh, Jenny," he sighed. The towel had dropped off her head. He ran his hands through her wet hair. She moved close, clinging to him.

"Stay," she whispered.

"Rick," Bob said, spoiling the moment. He put on his coat and left.

As the door closed Rick came out of his bedroom. "He's finally gone."

Jennifer reached for her brush and began untangling her still wet hair. "Not now, Rick, please. It's too late and I'm just too damned tired."

She ran into her bedroom and slammed the door behind her.

Lisa got into bed with her copy of Shakespeare. She adjusted the light and felt very pleased with her plan to educate herself. "Won't Bob be impressed when I can quote this stuff?" she said to herself.

She opened the heavy book and read from *The Taming of the Shrew*.

> A woman mov'd like a fountain troubled—
> Muddy, ill seeming, thick bereft of beauty
> And while it is so, none so dry or thirsty
> Will deign to sip or touch one drop of it.
> Thy husband is thy lord, thy life, thy keeper . . .

She thought a moment. "Shakespeare sure knew what he was talking about."

Putting the book down, she turned off the light. The night was very lonely.

Chapter Four
Love's Rocky Road

The storm began with rain which gradually turned to sleet and then finally to snow, leaving the roads treacherous and covered with ice. A travel alert had been issued.

Tom and Meredith had planned to get away for the weekend, to Loon Lodge, a small resort in upper Michigan. It was late Friday afternoon, and Tom looked out his office window and frowned. He picked up the phone and dialed Meredith's number.

She answered cheerily. "All packed and rarin' to go."

"I don't think so, Merry. Have you taken a look out there? It's turning into a real blizzard."

"Oh, come on, Tom. You won't let a little bad weather stop us. Why, in Switzerland this would be considered a light shower."

"This isn't Switzerland," he said soberly. "It's really bad."

"I can't stay in Oakdale another minute," she whined. "If I don't get out of this dreary place, I'll just shrivel up."

"Okay," Tom said. "We'll talk about it when I get home."

"Don't forget to bring an extra blanket, and pick up a bottle of champagne for the road."

The snow plows had just cleared the street in front of the apartment house, and Tom's car barely made it over the mounds of snow into the underground garage. He didn't know why, but he had stopped for the champagne. The parking lot at Bunbury's had been inaccessible because of the snow and he hadn't bought the extra blanket Meredith had wanted.

She greeted him with a juicy kiss and her flesh felt hot against his cold skin. He reached around her, and she quickly pulled away.

"Yuck, you're all wet and cold!"

"I told you it was miserable out there."

"I've got everything packed. No use taking off your coat. Let's leave now."

"Are you crazy?"

"Uh huh, and you love it. We'll probably have the whole place to ourselves." She ran her hand sensuously up his cheek and lightly bit his ear.

He closed his eyes, envisioning the lodge, a roaring fire, and complete privacy. There would be no Lisa to nag him, no family watching over his shoulder, no grandfather in the law office hounding him. There would be just the two of them.

He picked up her suitcase, slung his carry-all over his shoulder, and grabbed the bag with the champagne. Meredith carried a blanket from Tom's bed, two pillows, and her fur coat.

"Sure you can carry all of that?" he asked.

She nodded, balanced the load and followed cheerily

behind him.

He had to make one more trip to pick up his suitcase and the food she'd packed to eat in the car. By the time he was done the little red Mustang was fully loaded. "Looks like we're going away for a month," Tom said as he pulled out of the garage and bumped his way over the hills of snow.

"Maybe we will," Meredith said happily. "Who knows?"

Tom laughed. With Meredith around, there really was no telling what would come next. That's what he loved about her. Before they'd met, everything in his life had been orderly and predictable. She was like the storm, constantly changing, exciting, and dangerous. He found new adventure each time he was with her.

Before he pulled out onto the highway, he stopped the car and buckled his seat belt then looked over at Meredith, indicating she should do the same.

"You know I hate to use them," she reminded him. "They're too constraining."

"Do it for me," Tom pleaded. "This is a hell of a night."

She complied, but not without complaining.

The highway was empty. "No one in their right mind is out tonight," Tom said, gripping the wheel tightly. He could hardly see through the blowing snow.

"Who said we were sane?" Meredith asked. She reached over to kiss him on the nose, and the car skidded.

"Hey!" he shouted. "Not now, you'll get us killed."

Meredith sat back pouting, but after a few seconds she cheered and dug into the food she'd packed. "How about some crackers and cheese?" She spread some soft

Brie onto a cracker and stuffed it into Tom's mouth, distracting him.

The car skidded again. Tom tried to keep them on a straight course, but the road was too icy. The headlights of an approaching car seemed very close. He turned the steering wheel too quickly and the car began to spin. Tom fought desperately for control but they landed in a ditch, perched at a sharp angle. Tom had to strain to see Meredith.

"You okay?"

"I hurt my wrist when I tried to keep from lurching forward." She spoke soberly, realizing just how close they'd come to disaster. "If it weren't for the seat belt, I might have been killed."

Tom pushed against his door, but it was jammed. The door on Meredith's side was crushed against the snow. "We're not out of this yet. I can't get the door open. We're stuck in here."

Her eyes widened with fear. "But we have to get out! It's freezing."

Tom turned the engine off so they wouldn't asphyxiate, and struggled over the seat to reach for the blanket and Meredith's fur coat. "Here, we'll wrap up in these. Somebody's bound to come by."

"Only if they're crazy." Meredith's voice cracked with fear.

Tom wrapped the blanket around them and pulled Meredith against him, trying his best to comfort her as the storm raged.

"How'd you get away?" Bob asked when Jennifer joined him at the Oakdale Inn for dinner.

"I just decided it was finally time to bite the bullet,"

she said.

"And Rick?"

"He'll be at the hospital all night. There've been all kinds of accidents tonight."

"I wouldn't have blamed you if you'd canceled. It's beastly out."

"Our apartment isn't far from here. I walked."

"But the wind chill is—"

"Better than taking the car."

He agreed. "I'm not sure I'll be able to make it home tonight. Think I'll take a room here."

"Good idea," she said as she peeked over the menu. "Maybe you should too."

She looked at Bob thoughtfully for a moment and smiled. "Maybe I should."

After dinner, they registered, taking separate rooms. Then Bob, called home and the hospital to tell them he was staying at the Oakdale Inn for the night because of the weather. When he hung up he joined Jennifer in her room.

The Oakdale Inn was known for its rustic charm. The rooms were decorated in colonial fashion, with handmade quilts on authentic maple four-poster beds. Federal blue wallpaper with a small white print covered the walls, and cheerful fabric in a warm pink covered the chairs.

"This room suits you," Bob said. "Warm, lovely, a little old fashioned."

"I'm not old fashioned enough to have resisted being here," she reminded him.

"I'm glad of that," he said, smiling.

Jennifer kissed Bob lightly on the lips, savoring the taste of him. His dark eyes sparkled, and his arms felt warm and comforting.

Theirs wasn't a love of quick passion, but of a tender nature, gentle and caring. It was a special kind of love which, like fine wine, had to be savored.

The phone rang, awakening both Jennifer and Bob simultaneously. He reached for it as she turned on the light and looked at him questioningly.

"Probably the hospital. I told the desk clerk to call me here," he explained, picking up the receiver. "Hello," he answered.

"Bob!"

"Lisa? What the h—"

"It's Tom, there's been an accident. I'm at Memorial." Jennifer saw Bob's face blanch. "Is he all right?"

"Frostbite, and I don't know what else. Bob, please— we need you."

"I'm on my way." He jumped out of the bed. "Tom's been hurt. I've gotta go."

"Think you'll make it through the snow?"

"I have to." He looked at his watch. It was only five A.M. "Try to get back to sleep."

"Be careful," Jennifer said as he left.

"I will." He threw her a kiss and closed the door softly behind him.

Tom was resting comfortably in a bed at Memorial when Bob finally got back to Lisa. She was pacing the hallway nervously, and Mom and Dad Hughes were sitting worriedly in the visitor's lounge.

"He's okay," Bob announced. "Exposure, a few minor bruises, and a bit shaken. He was pretty scared."

"Are you sure he's all right?"

"Positive," Bob said, reaching for Lisa's hand to reassure her.

"What was he doing out in that terrible storm?"

"Seems he and Meredith were going to Loon Lodge."

"All the way up there in this weather?" Nancy asked.

"Seems so."

"And the girl, is she all right?"

"Mom, I think she would probably survive a fall off a steep cliff. There's something very resilient about her. Besides suffering from exposure, she's got a badly sprained wrist and some painful bruises, but she's already chafing to get out of the hospital."

"I knew she was a disaster," Lisa said. "Wait'll I talk to Tom."

"Lisa's right," Chris said. "If it weren't for that wicked girl . . ."

"Tom had something to do with this too," Bob reminded them. "Let's wait until he's recovered a little before we begin the campaign again, please."

"Bob, there are times I think you're just too patient," Lisa said.

"Maybe we balance each other, Lisa."

"You've got a point there. Can I see him?"

"He's bushed and probably sleeping, but it won't do any harm for you to be there."

Lisa sighed with relief and kissed Bob thankfully before going to Tom's room.

Jennifer and Rick arrived home at the same time. "Mom? Where've you been. I tried calling you and no one answered."

"I went out to dinner with Bob," she replied.

"And you're just getting home now?"

"Maybe you haven't noticed, but there was a terrible storm last night. I decided to stay at the Inn rather than braving the weather."

"And Bob stayed too, I bet."

"Separate rooms," Jennifer snapped back. "You can check the registry."

"I'll bet," Rick said sourly.

"Rick Ryan!" Jennifer said angrily. "I don't have to make any excuses for my social life. Do you understand that?"

"Dad's hardly cold and you're already getting serious about someone else. I guess that shows how much you really loved him!"

"That's nonsense, Rick. I loved your father very much and you know it! It's just because I loved him so, that I love Bob."

"Sure," Rick said, unconvinced. He stormed up to his room and slammed the door.

There was no time for an argument. Jennifer took a shower, dressed in her nurse's uniform, and left for the hospital, all the while hoping, for Bob's sake, that his son was all right.

The storm had ended and the roads to Oakdale were open again. Although she had hardly been able to sleep all night, Lisa got up early and headed for the hospital to see Tom.

He was sitting up in bed eating breakfast when she entered.

"You really had us worried, young man," she scolded. "Imagine being so foolish as to take off in such a storm. Whatever possessed you to behave so irrationally?" She knew it had to be Meredith, but chose not to bring her up so soon after coming to see him.

"It wasn't so bad, Mom."

"Not bad?" She handed Tom a copy of the morning paper. A picture of the wrecked car was on the front page. "You call this not bad?"

"Looks worse than it was."

"If that trucker hadn't been out last night, you'd have frozen to death."

"But we didn't."

"We're really fine," Meredith said, coming in behind Lisa.

"Really!" Lisa ripped the paper from Tom's hand and thrust it at Meredith. "Tom Hughes, if you weren't bigger than me, I'd turn you over my knee."

"An appropriate reaction," a deep baritone voice said. "Maybe a spanking would help."

Meredith turned pale. "Simon! What are you doing here?" she demanded, turning toward the door.

A man entered the room and read from a copy of the newspaper he was holding.

" 'Meredith Halliday, a new resident of Oakdale, and Thomas Christopher Hughes, son of Dr. Robert Hughes and Lisa Hughes, were rescued from their wrecked and stranded vehicle early this morning by Herman Glockstein, a local trucker.' You made the newspaper, dear."

"I guess I did," Meredith mumured contritely. "So you found me."

"I always do," Simon said. "You know I always do, sweetheart."

Lisa listened to their conversation attentively, but she never took her eyes off the man. He was spectacular, like nothing Oakdale had ever seen before. Tall and dark, he was wearing a dark blue woolen sports jacket. His dark eyes were intelligent and his mouth sensuous. She wanted to touch him to see if he was real.

When he spoke to Lisa his deep voice softened. "Simon Gilby," he said as he extended his hand.

Lisa smiled demurely. "Lisa Shea. I'm Tom's mother."

"You were right to chastize your son. I've come to do the same to Meredith," he said. "I see we think alike."

"I—I guess so," Lisa said, completely taken aback. She looked to Meredith, then to Simon, wondering about their relationship.

God, please, she thought. *Don't let him be her sugar daddy.*

It was a dismal evening—dark, cold, and wet—and it matched Lisa's mood perfectly. She'd given up on Shakespeare and was trying to force her way through Dickens, when the phone rang. Any distraction was welcome, and she leapt eagerly for the phone.

"Lisa, Simon Gilby here. We met at the hospital."

It was the voice she had hoped to hear. *Be calm Lisa. Don't frighten him off*, she told herself. "Why, Mister Gilby how nice of you to call." She thought it politic to ask after Meredith and forced the question. "How is Meredith doing?"

"Simon, please," the pleasant voice said.

"Simon," she repeated, liking the sound of his name.

"That's better. I knew you'd be concerned about her. Meredith's shaken, but she's recovering quickly. She's never down for long. Ever since her parents died and I became her guardian, she's been a challenge."

"You're her guardian. I see," Lisa said. A feeling of relief washed over her. "She's certainly a live wire." She thought that was a reasonably polite thing to say about Meredith. There was no use telling him the truth.

"Would you like to have dinner with me tomorrow evening?"

"Well . . . " She purposely hesitated. "I think I can get away. Let me look at my calendar." Lisa took a few deep breaths, waited about thirty seconds, then spoke again. "It seems I'm free." She tried not to sound too eager. "I'd love to."

"I'll pick you up at eight."

After she gave him her address, Lisa hung up and searched through her closet for something appropriate to wear. "Something a bit tailored, but not dowdy," she said to herself. "Maybe green or blue . . . There's just nothing right," she said finally. "I'd better get over to Bunbury's to pick up something."

Jennifer had just come out of a patient's room when Bob bumped into her. "We've gotta stop meeting this way," he joked.

"I heard Tom's all right," she said. "I wanted to get down to see him, but—"

"Duty called. I understand."

"Mrs. Ryan," John Dixon called as he walked down the hall. John looked the picture of efficiency in his spotless white hospital coat. His straight blond hair was neatly combed, although a small cowlick stubbornly rose from the center. His blue eyes were cold. "Mrs. Ryan, don't you have some medication to administer?"

"I'm headed for the drug room now," she said, turning and silently saying goodbye to Bob.

Bob followed her into the drug room and watched her measure out a prescription. "Seriously, Jennifer, I want to spend all of my time with you."

"But, Bob, it's too soon after Sean's death."

"Do you really believe that? Do you think Sean would want you to be alone?"

"What about Rick?"

"What about him? He's a grown man. He's almost finished with his residency and ready to go out on his own. He's more than capable of taking care of himself. I know now I made a mistake when I recommended that he be able to finish his residency here. He said he wanted to move to Oakdale so you wouldn't be alone. But you needn't ever be alone again. Marry me, Jenny. Let's spend the rest of our nights like last night, in each other's arms."

Rick's reaction that morning had disturbed Jennifer greatly, more than she'd even admitted to herself. But she knew she couldn't let her son run her life, especially since she'd fallen in love with Bob Hughes. Bob was an extraordinary man. She wanted to leap into his arms, but she had to give it some consideration before responding. "I can't give you an answer now, Bob," she forced herself to say. "I need time to think it over."

"Can I see you tonight at the Inn?"

"We can't make a habit of—"

"Just to talk, Jenny."

"I'll meet you after my shift. Five-thirty all right?"

"Any time I can be with you is all right with me."

Jenny was still wearing her uniform when she met Bob in the lobby of the Inn.

"Dinner?" he asked.

"I don't think so. Not tonight."

They went into the bar and chose a quiet corner.

"Did you think over what I said this morning?" Bob asked eagerly.

"Uh huh . . ."

"Well, are you going to keep me guessing?"

She laughed. "You're like a little boy sometimes, Bob. Maybe that's why I love you so much."

"Then you do love me."

"Who wouldn't? You're gentle and kind and sensitive and loving. There's nothing more a woman could want."

"How about a knight in shining armor riding a white charger and sweeping you off your lovely feet?"

"*You* are my knight, Bob. You rescued me from what could have been a nightmare when Sean died."

"And will you be my lady?" he asked, taking her hand in his.

She leaned over the table and kissed him. "You bet I will."

"Soon?" Bob asked, smiling broadly.

"As soon as you'd like. At our age, being coy is not too practical."

"How about in two weeks?" he suggested.

She poked through her purse and looked at a small calendar in her wallet. "Two weeks, on a Sunday. Bob, that's the week before Christmas."

"We can take a short honeymoon over the holidays. The Bahamas?"

"Warm sunshine, beaches, no snow. You've got a date, Bob Hughes!" Jennifer promised, throwing her arms around Bob for an affectionate hug.

Simon was everything Lisa had imagined he would be. He picked her up in a blue Rolls Royce Silver Cloud, ordered dinner in French, and knew all the best wines. After the meal he ordered cheese and fruit and a dessert wine, which Lisa thought was wonderful.

Lisa looked around the elegant dining room at the Inn to see if anyone was staring at them. He was so handsome, so commanding, she was sure she had to be the envy of every woman there. His white silk monogrammed shirt showed under a dark silk suit, and his tie, a deep red with a hint of a blue stripe, set the whole thing off perfectly. She'd never met a man who dressed so meticulously.

Lisa was glad she'd decided to buy a new dress for the occasion. Nothing she had owned would have been quite right. Lisa's dress was a tasteful emerald green crepe. She had chosen to wear just a simple gold chain and earrings. The green gown enhanced the color of her eyes, making them shine with vitality. She silently congratulated herself for her decision to dress more conservatively than usual.

"You look lovely this evening," he said, lifting his crystal wine glass toward her in a toast.

She wanted to say, "You do too," but held back, smiling her acknowledgment instead.

"Will you be staying in Oakdale long?" she asked hopefully.

"As long as it takes to get Meredith pried loose."

Lisa couldn't help but let a little sarcastic tinge creep into her voice. "That might take considerable time. She seems to be very smitten by Tom."

"Do I detect a note of disapproval?" Simon asked.

Lisa didn't know whether he wanted her to say "yes" or "no", so she simply smiled.

"I see," Simon said, his broad grin displaying a set of

white even teeth. "You don't think much of their seeing each other either."

Lisa was relieved. He seemed to feel the same way she did about the affair. Maybe Simon could help her get Meredith's claws out of Tom.

"Actually, I have a favor to ask of you, Lisa. I hope I'm not presuming too much."

"Depends on what it is."

"Will you help me convince Meredith to return home?"

"I've been working at that for quite some time with very little success," Lisa admitted.

"But together we may be able to whip up some plan that will do the trick."

Lisa loved intrigue. She leaned closer to him, waiting to hear more.

Jennifer sat in her living room ready to go to her wedding. Two weeks had flown by and she had barely managed to find time to do half the things necessary. She knew few people in Oakdale, so Nancy had helped. Although she didn't yet know them well, Jennifer was growing very fond of Bob's family. They had made her feel comfortable from the beginning, and when she and Bob had announced their engagement, the Hughes family had been overwhelmingly receptive.

Rick walked quickly through the living room and disappeared into his room without even glancing at his mother.

Jennifer shouted after him. "You still have time to change your mind, Rick. Bob really wants you to be best man."

"Forget it," Rick shouted back. "I'm not that easy to

buy off."

"I can't understand you, Rick. Don't you want me to be happy?"

"Sure I do. But not when you betray my father."

"I'm not betraying him. I loved him."

"You sure have a funny way of showing it. He's hardly cold and you're getting married again!"

She followed Rick into his bedroom and sat down on the bed. "Let me try to explain," she began wearily.

He turned his back. "I don't want to hear it, Mom."

"I don't care what you want! You'll listen to me, Rick Ryan, whether you like it or not! Your father and I were married for over twenty-five happy years. I never wanted another man, and I know he never had another woman. We were fortunate. Not many people are so lucky. When he died I was desolate, and Bob was there to help. Bob is kind and caring. He's very much like your father was. I had a good marriage and I'm not afraid to chance another. Once grief passes all that's left is loneliness, Rick, and I don't want to be alone for the rest of my life. It honors your father that we had such a good relationship and that he made me so secure that I can look forward to another."

Rick's fists were clenched and his mouth was a hardened line.

"Aren't you going to wish me luck today?" Jennifer asked, hoping to soften him.

Rick turned to her, his eyes shining, brimming with unshed tears. But he didn't say another word to comfort his mother.

The doorbell rang. It was Donald, come to pick Jennifer up to bring her to the Hughes house for the wedding. Jennifer quickly glanced back at her son's closed door, then left with Donald.

The living room at the Hughes home was decorated festively. With Christmas and the wedding coinciding, Nancy had gone all out. Red and white candles with sprays of evergreen covered the mantle. Candles were everywhere, lit and flickering. The fireplace blazed, warming the cold midwestern winter afternoon. The Christmas tree was beautiful, decorated with homemade ornaments Nancy had collected or made through the years. The tree was dotted with hundreds of tiny lights, all glowing softly, and ornaments that had been made when each of the four Hughes children were born. There was also one for Tom—and even one for Lisa. Bob's other marriage was commemorated with an ornament for Sandy. They had been part of the family and Nancy hadn't removed them from the tree. A new, miniature pink gingham doll with Jennifer's name embroidered on it had joined the other ornaments this year. Nancy liked Jennifer and hoped Bob would finally find happiness with her.

Nancy watched Bob greeting the guests, and smiled. He was such a good son. Then Tom entered, and Nancy couldn't help but think how handsome her grandson had turned out to be. She saw the bandage still covering his bruised forehead and was grateful the accident hadn't been more serious. Meredith came in behind Tom and Nancy's smile faded.

That girl! Nancy thought. *How could he bring her?* She steeled herself, smiled once more and greeted Meredith as if she were a welcome guest.

No one was more surprised than Nancy when Carol showed up at the wedding. She looked lovely in a simple green velvet dress decorated with a red and green plaid bow. Nancy watched Carol join Tom and Meredith.

"Thanks for inviting me, Tom. I really like your father and wouldn't have missed this occasion for anything."

Meredith looked at Carol as if she had the plague. Tom introduced the two women.

The entire series of events didn't go unnoticed by either Nancy or Chris Hughes, who both wondered how Carol could be civil to Meredith or to Tom, after he'd dropped her in favor of the other woman. But Carol smiled through it all, and actually seemed forgiving.

Lisa made an unforgettable entrance. Escorted by Simon Gilby, who looked like a modern version of Prince Charming, Bob's ex-wife was a glittering Cinderella. The tapered hem of her bead covered rose-pink dress sparkled with matching sequins, and her hat was an astonishing creation of sequins and pink pearls. Lisa swept into the house, greeting everyone a little too cheerfully.

How she could have come at all amazed Chris and Nancy. It was almost unheard of for an ex-wife to attend her former husband's wedding. They never expected her to accept the invitation, sent out of politeness. But then Lisa was well known for doing the unusual.

Jennifer had been shepherded upstairs through the back door, so that Bob couldn't see his bride before the wedding. Donald gave her time to change clothes, then went downstairs and told the minister the ceremony could begin. Everyone took their places. Tom switched on the stereo and the wedding march began to play.

Bob turned to see Jennifer walk down the stairs, her right hand lightly resting on his father's arm. They stopped at his side. Chris took Jennifer's hand and put it on Bob's, then stepped back.

Bob thought his bride was the most beautiful creature in the world. She looked wondrous. Her periwinkle blue silk suit and hat, brimmed with matching silk flowers, set off her sparkling azure eyes. She was beaming, and her smile warmed him to the soul. He'd never been so happy.

It was a traditional ceremony. Donald, delighted for Bob, stood up for his brother. Handing Bob the rings, he wondered if he ever could find such happiness himself.

Once the vows were completed and the rings exchanged, Bob kissed his wife.

As everyone was congratulating the newlyweds, the door opened and a cold wind blasted through the room.

It was Rick.

Disheveled, obviously drunk and hostile, he entered like a storm. His speech was slurred as he reeled toward his mother. "So you did it. Hardly buried one and married another."

Chris took hold of Rick's arm. "Come upstairs with me. You're drunk."

"You're damn right, I'm drunk. I'm celebrating my mother's wedding. But then you know that. Look at her, that *bride* over there. At least she didn't wear white!"

Don grabbed Rick's other arm, trying to assist Chris. But Rick wouldn't be stopped. He pulled away and lurched toward Jennifer.

"You couldn't wait. Had to find another one right away. I hope you're cursed forever. Both of you."

"Rick," Jennifer cried. "Oh, God, Rick, please try to understand. It's not like that at all . . . "

Rick grabbed Jennifer's arm, pulling her away from Bob. "Oh, I understand all right. You'll both regret this. That I promise you!"

Bob rescued Jennifer as Don and Chris took Rick aside.

"That's enough!" Don shouted as he latched onto Rick's arm. "Upstairs with you and sleep it off." He and Chris pushed the drunken young man toward the stairs.

"He'll be all right, Jennifer," Chris assured her. "He'll feel differently when he sobers up."

After much commotion, Donald, Chris and Bob managed to subdue Rick and lead him to a bedroom upstairs.

Once they were gone, Jennifer burst into tears. Carol took over as hostess, filling in for the distressed Hugheses until some semblance of calm could be reestablished.

Nancy kept Jennifer company as she changed her clothes. Although she had finally stopped crying, Jen looked stricken and pale.

"We'll take good care of Rick," Nancy assured her new daughter-in-law. "He'll be fine with us. I promise."

As they drove to a small inn just north of Oakdale, Jennifer began to cry again. Bob was at a loss as to how to console her.

"I'm so sorry, Bob. I've tried everything with Rick. I had no idea he'd go so far."

"Mom and Dad have managed worse characters. I'm sure they'll straighten him out. Let's just try to enjoy the moment. There will be plenty of time to deal with problems later."

She tried to smile as he took her hand in his and gave it a squeeze. Jennifer looked out the window at the passing rural landscape. The world looked white and clean; everything looked fresh and new. Perhaps it was a new beginning for her.

She nuzzled close to him. "I love you, Bob Hughes."

He grinned and pulled her closer. "And I love you too, Mrs. Hughes, more than anyone in the world."

Chapter Five

Deception

Lisa swished across the room, trailing the feathered end of a jade green peignoir behind her. She knew Simon was watching and grinned when he whistled at her.

"Lady, you are the most elegant creature I've met in a long time," he said as she lay down beside him on the bed.

"You're not so bad yourself. Oakdale sure needed someone like you." *I needed someone like you,* was what she really meant. She tousled his thick dark hair, enjoying the silkiness of it.

Simon is as far from the boring and pawing Tod Jory, as the earth is to the stars, she thought. Simon was a star, brightening her future prospects, and she sure didn't mind being caught in his orbit.

Simon took her gently into his arms and kissed her. It was wonderful being with a gentleman, and a rich one too. Lisa sighed contentedly. Life was looking up.

Simon admired Lisa's slim figure, shown to complete advantage by her sheer nightgown. A strap dropped and he kissed her bare shoulder, making her shiver with delight. She pulled him closer.

Even the thought of him was thrilling; his touch was electric, sending currents of pleasure through her every nerve. He was an exciting and gentle lover, but just a touch selfish, requiring satisfaction and not much worrying about hers. It didn't matter. Lisa was more than satisfied; she was ecstatic.

"Lisa," he said, kissing her lightly once again. "It's time we put our plan into action."

She lay beside him, her head on his chest, gazing at the ceiling. If Simon had asked her at that moment to murder her mother, she probably would have.

The thought of being away from him for even a moment brought her back to reality. "Now?"

"Tomorrow. I thought you wanted to get Meredith out of your son's life as much as I want to get her back home where she belongs. She's been playing around long enough."

Lisa thought of the accident and agreed. "That beautiful new car was totaled, wasn't it?"

"I'm sure she's out shopping for another," Simon replied without too much concern.

"But it was brand new."

"The insurance company will handle it. As long as no one was hurt, the car really is of little significance."

Lisa wished she could be so unconcerned about money. Maybe, if she played her cards right with Simon, she could be.

Early the next morning Lisa packed and was on her way to New York. After an argument with the cab driver about going to Brooklyn, she found the address Simon had given her. She couldn't find a doorbell.

With a cautious glance down the hall, she knocked on the door of the stranger's apartment. When no one answered, she knocked again, louder and more persistently.

"Yeah, coming," someone grumbled. "Hold yer horses."

She heard the rattle of a chain and then the click of a lock opening. "Yeah, wad do ya want?"

Lisa was stunned. Standing in front of her, wearing just a small terry towel around his hips, was the most attractive young man she'd ever seen. His chiseled features displayed a look of chagrin. "Well, are ya gonna stand there with your mouth open, or are ya gonna tell me what ya want?"

"I—uh—Simon Gilby sent me."

"Why didn't ya say so in the first place. Come on in." He opened the door wider.

Lisa peeked in, trying to decide whether it was wise to enter the apartment.

"Ya gonna wait 'till next Christmas, Lady. The hallway's freezin', in case ya didn't notice."

She realized he must have been chilled to the bone and stepped in.

"It's about time," he said, rubbing his arms briskly. "I was beginnin' to freeze."

Lisa could see the goose bumps on his fair flesh. He wasn't exaggerating. "Wait a minute," he said, disappearing into another room. When he returned he had put on a pair of very tight jeans and an Erin knit sweater. He was blond, so blond his rather thick eyebrows were almost lost. Lisa found herself staring into his eyes, which were a startling shade of violet.

Contact lenses, she thought at first, but he'd

obviously just come out of the shower when he'd answered the door and couldn't possibly have been wearing any. No, his violet eyes had to be natural.

Lisa found it difficult to talk to this young Adonis. She felt as if she were speaking to a Michaelangelo sculpture. He didn't seem real. "Simon told me to give you this," she said, handing him a small envelope.

He opened it and whistled when he finished counting out ten, one thousand dollar bills. "Must be some job!"

Lisa gasped when she saw the money. *Ten thousand dollars! Simon must really want Meredith to leave Oakdale for him to put out that much money,* she thought.

She had no idea she had been carrying so much cash and was rather grateful she'd not given into temptation and opened the envelope. The fact that Simon had insisted payment be in cash, rather than with a check, bothered her just a touch.

"I want no written evidence of this little deal," he said when he'd handed her the envelope. "And I want no connection with the person you're going to meet."

"What about me?" she'd asked.

"No one could connect you with him. Don't worry, he's done favors for me before."

Lisa couldn't help but wonder what kind of favors as she explained Simon's plan to the young man. When she was done she realized she didn't even know his name. "I'm Lisa—"

"Stop right there," he said. "No names. The boss prefers it that way."

"But what should I call you?"

"Buz."

After she'd left, Lisa wondered why Simon would be

so secretive, and who Buz really was. After hearing the young man's somewhat inarticulate speech she wondered if he would be able to carry out the plan. It would take someone sophisticated and suave to lure Meredith away from Tom. Good looks may not be enough. She wondered why Simon had picked Buz for the job.

John Dixon knew he had an audience to watch him perform surgery. He thrived on attention and encouraged it. He looked up at the glass viewing window above the operating room and spoke through his mask. "This procedure is new and rather risky. It was strongly indicated by the patient's declining condition. I believe the risk factor is overcome by the prospective result. Her chances of survival are about forty percent, but without the surgery her life expectancy is only a month, possibly two."

He extended his hand to the nurse who slapped a scalpel into it. John slowly and confidently made a deep cut directly across the patient's chest. His surgical team was well rehearsed and moved through the critical procedure without any wasted motion.

Bob, watching from the viewing room, had to admit the man was an absolute genius with the scalpel, but John's showmanship bothered him. A woman's life was at stake and he was performing as if he were on a stage.

"Impressive," Lee Stokes, the Hospital Administrator said. "He's a real asset to Memorial."

"He's very talented," Bob responded noncommittally.

Later, after the patient had been taken to the recovery room, John met with the doctors who had observed the surgery. It was as if he were holding court, Bob thought and wondered if two heart specialists were one too many for Memorial.

Later that afternoon, Bob headed up to C.C.U. to check on one of his patients and on the progress of John's surgical patient as well. He could hear John's shouting before he even entered the unit.

"What the hell did you think you were doing?"

Close to tears, Jennifer, held a chart up to John.

"I followed your orders, Doctor."

"What's the problem," Bob demanded as he hurried through the glass doors.

"Morphine every three hours!" John bellowed. "What were you trying to do?"

Bob took the chart from Jennifer and read the orders: Morphine Q 3-4 hrs. PRN for pain.

These directions weren't unusual for patients who had just undergone surgery. Morphine was the usual drug indicated under the circumstances and the orders were that it should be administered every three to four hours.

"But your orders said every three to four hours, Dr. Dixon."

"I meant four," John raged. "Don't you have any sense at all? Every three hours is too much. You're completely incompetent. I'm going to report you to the Director of Nursing."

"Wait a minute," Bob broke in. "You don't have to get abusive."

"You stay out of this," John snapped, grabbing the chart from Bob. "It's none of your concern."

"When someone is shouting at my wife, it definitely

78

does concern me," Bob said, standing between John and Jennifer.

"This has nothing to do with your wife. It concerns a medical procedure. It's between a nurse and a doctor."

"That's right," Bob said angrily, "and as a member of the staff I won't tolerate your badgering any nurse."

"Well that's just too bad, Dr. Hughes. Maybe it's time you come down a notch and realize you don't have the final say around here anymore."

Bob was so infuriated he lunged threateningly at John.

"Bob!" Jennifer screamed, trying to hold him back. "It's not worth it. We'll hash it out. I'll be all right."

Jennifer's voice calmed him and Bob turned and led her from the room. He stalked down the hall, furious at himself for losing his temper, and even angrier at John for provoking him.

Chapter Six
The Lovely Lady

Meredith drove to the Oakdale Inn and handed the parking attendant the keys to her new Porsche. "What a lucky accident," she told herself, as she watched the car drive off. "This one's much better than the Mustang." She breezed into the lobby and checked for mail. Now that Simon had discovered where she was there had been no need for keeping her whereabouts a secret anymore, so she'd called friends. "Why did he have to come here?" she fretted. "I'm having such a good time slumming. Now he wants me to go back to that dreary old house where he can watch me every minute. I'll show him. I'll marry Tom and buy a house on the Riviera, or on a Greek island. Maybe I'll buy the *entire* island. . . ."

Just as the elevator doors were about to close, a young man made a mad dash toward it, running right into Meredith.

"I'm so sorry," he said, helping her recover. "Are you hurt?"

Meredith rubbed her bruised arm. "Why don't you

look where you're going," she said angrily. Then she looked up at the man. He was incredibly handsome, with blond hair, even features, a full mouth, and startling violet eyes.

The elevator door closed, confining them in the cubicle alone. "I'd like to make it up to you, Miss . . . Would you have dinner with me this evening?"

"Halliday," she answered, "Meredith Halliday."

He offered his hand. "Gregory Peters. I just arrived from New York."

"One of my favorite places," Meredith said. "I love the shopping."

"The very best," he agreed, "except for London, of course." The elevator stopped and she started to get out. He held the door open. "Dinner?"

"Sorry, I'm busy tonight."

"Some other time, then?"

"Maybe," she teased as she went down the hall.

He looked after her, noted what room she'd gone to, then allowed the doors to close.

Meredith was dressed for dinner with Tom. Just as she was about to leave there was a knock on her door. A delivery boy, nearly hidden by flowers, stood in the doorway. "Miss Halliday?"

She nodded.

"These are for you." He handed her the largest bouquet she'd ever seen. She tipped him generously, and when he'd gone, opened the note.

To Meredith with my apologies, Greg.
P.S. Tomorrow evening. 7 P.M.
Suite 1101
* * *

82

Tanned and relaxed, Bob and Jennifer had returned from the Bahamas. The mail was piled high and Jennifer attacked it the first chance she got. She was stacking up the bills, when she found a personal letter. She opened it eagerly, read it, then jumped out of her seat, ran over to Bob and hugged him tight.

"Hey, I thought the honeymoon was over," he teased. "What prompted that?"

"My sister is coming. She couldn't make the wedding, but she says she can get away now." She reread the letter quickly. "Oh, Bob, she's arriving today! It says January 30. Midwest Airlines, Flight 426, 9:45." She looked up at the antique clock Grandpa Hughes had given them as a wedding present. "We'll hardly make it to the airport in time."

Jennifer was as excited as a child at Christmas. She'd been disappointed when her sister hadn't been able to be maid of honor at their wedding, but had never told Bob much about her.

"There she is. Oh, Bob, there she is!" Jennifer shouted. Bob watched her run to a tall, conservatively dressed dark haired woman. "Bob, I want you to meet Kim," Jennifer called after embracing her sister.

Kim smiled sweetly, and the corners of her eyes crinkled. "Bob. It's so nice to meet you. Jennifer's letters have extolled you beyond belief, but now that I've met you I can understand why."

Bob couldn't help staring. Never had he seen a more appealing person. She had nearly bowled him over with her charm, and he had hardly met her.

He watched the two sisters walking in front of him, chatting away as they headed for the baggage area. Bob wondered how one family could have been blessed with two such wonderful women.

Dinner with Greg Peters proved to be quite an experience for Meredith. He was very attentive and gave her a corsage of sterling silver roses. She knew they were impossible to get without some trouble and expense in the midwest wintertime. He had spared no expense. Fresh Maine lobsters had been flown in for the occasion, and the caviar was real Beluga. They drank the finest French champagne, and after dinner sipped fine old Napoleon brandy.

Greg was wearing an elegant hand-tailored tuxedo. Unobtrusively in the background, a violinist played a romantic gypsy tune. When Meredith met his gaze, he smiled and began to play a sweet, classical melody.

The dinner she'd had with Tom the night before paled in comparison to her evening with Greg. The collision with this mysterious stranger in the elevator was well worth the sore spot on her arm. He was the most fascinating man Meredith had ever met.

The next week when Simon invited Lisa to dinner, she was astonished to find that Meredith and a transformed Buz would accompany them. He now called himself Gregory Peters and she knew that name was probably as phony as the one he had given her. Lisa, enjoying the game, knew not to let on that she'd met the young man or that Simon had paid him all that money. Buz was a fine actor. No one could possibly have guessed he'd ever met either Lisa or Simon before. What was most surprising was the dramatic change in the young man. His speech was now flawless, even cultured, and his manners impeccable. It was hard to imagine he was the same rather tasteless creature she'd seen in New York. Now she understood why Simon had hired him. He was a chameleon, able to change his colors at will.

When she arrived home that night, Tom was waiting there for her. "Mom, I just have to talk to you," he announced.

"Tom, I'm really bushed," she said, stripping her white fox jacket off and tossing it on the couch.

"It's Meredith. I haven't been able to get through to her for three days. She keeps making excuses."

"Well maybe she's busy."

"Has Simon said anything to you about her?" he asked in a low voice.

Lisa hesitated a moment. Should she tell Tom about Greg or let Meredith do that? Should she pretend she hadn't had dinner with them? No. It wasn't worth it, she decided. "To be honest, Tom, I didn't know how to tell you this, but Meredith is seeing another young man."

"Why didn't you tell me?"

"I just found out tonight. Besides, it really isn't up to me to be the one to break the news to you. After all, I'm not involved in any of this," she said with total and convincing innocence.

"Do you think Meredith is serious about this guy?"

"Why don't you ask her, Tom?"

Bob Hughes's house had never been so lively. With Kim and Jennifer both there, there was a constant buzz of activity. One night Bob had one of Jennifer's aprons on, and was putting the finishing touches on his own special spicy spaghetti sauce, while Jennifer was dressing for dinner.

"*Voila*," Kim said, stepping back with the oven mitts still on her hands. "My creation is finished."

Bob examined the result of her efforts. "That's beautiful," he said, handing her the spoon for a taste of spaghetti sauce. "I never could understand how anyone could bake a cake. It looks delicious."

"It's easy." she said. "Just tread softly and pray a lot."

He laughed. "I don't think even prayer would work for me."

The Hughes family arrived in force. The coats were removed, and introductions made before Jennifer called them all to dinner.

There was someone obviously missing at the dinner table and Kim noticed. "Where's Rick?"

A momentary hush fell over the table, and everyone looked to Jennifer.

"He's busy at the hospital," she said simply and stared at her plate.

"I've been here two days and there hasn't been a word from that nephew of mine. I'm going to have to have a serious talk with him," Kim said lightly.

"Kim," Nancy said, breaking the tension. "Jennifer tells us you've been traveling in Europe."

"Yes, I have," she answered. "But it's so good to be back in the States. You don't know how much I missed even the simplest things. A clean restroom seems like a miracle, and I never believed a good juicy hamburger and french fries could taste so good."

Nancy laughed. "I think I understand, dear. There's really no place like home, is there?"

"No, indeed," Kim agreed. She turned her attention to Tom. "Have you and Rick gotten together much,

Tom?"

"Uh—well—no. I'm pretty busy at the law office, and he's usually working at Memorial . . ." Tom muttered, noticing the look of approval in his father's eyes.

The dinner was fun and festive and by the time everyone left they all agreed that Jennifer's sister, Kim, was a wonderful and rare person.

Bob and Jennifer went to bed that night feeling warm and contented. Except for the problem with Rick, which had mellowed some lately, their future looked wonderful.

When Tom arrived home he found Meredith sitting in front of the fireplace watching the late news. "Merry," he said with delight. "I haven't seen you in days."

She handed him a snifter of brandy. "I've been busy."

"That's obvious," he said, wondering how to broach the subject of the other man in her life.

"Tom, there's no use beating around the bush. I've met someone else. A man who matches my lifestyle and can afford me. I'm sure Simon will be delighted when he finds I don't have to spend my own money anymore. Greg and I have a very good arrangement. But there's no place in it for you, lamb. No place at all. It was fun while it lasted, though."

Tom was crushed. "Fun? Is that all it was for you?"

"Why of course. It never could have been anything more."

"I love you. You must know that. I want to marry you."

She laughed. "Marry? Tom, what ever would I want to do that for?"

"But I thought you loved me too."

"Don't be so naive. It was fun, a game. I like you, but I don't want to marry you—or anyone for that matter! You never could manage to satisfy me. After all, I have very expensive tastes."

His mouth hardened into a grim line as she spoke. He was too stunned to respond, too overwhelmed by the cavalier way in which she was ending their relationship. Tom watched helplessly as Meredith threw her seal jacket casually over her shoulders. She turned and waved before she closed the door.

The whole thing had started with her wave, he remembered sadly as he stood alone in the empty room.

"Well, Lisa, we did it," Simon said, raising his glass to her. "Meredith returned home with Greg."

"What'll she do when he leaves? Won't she suspect—"

"What, Meredith? What could she suspect? When he leaves, there'll be another. There always is. Meredith doesn't have much time for looking back." He sipped his wine. "Greg did his job well, don't you think?"

"Who is he?" she asked. "He was like two different people."

"It's best you don't know."

Lisa both liked and worried about Simon's secretiveness. He was a wonderful lover, was attentive and caring; and yet there was always a hint of something else, something mysterious and perhaps a little dangerous. Lisa had to admit that that was what attracted her to Simon most. He was a mystery she wanted very much to solve.

She smiled and sipped her champagne. "Now that Meredith's taken care of you can relax and we can enjoy some private moments again."

"I'll have to be leaving Oakdale," he said without losing his smile.

"Leave? When?"

"Tomorrow morning."

"But I thought . . ."

His smile was charming but no longer warm. "Lisa, it has been wonderful."

"Has been, Simon? We have so much in common. I thought . . ."

"Lisa, the only things we have in common are that we both like a good time and we both wanted Meredith and Tom to break up. We've had our lark, and Meredith is back where I want her. It's time for me to leave."

Lisa's lips parted, but there was nothing she could say. *You've used me*, she wanted to scream. *You never cared about me at all!*

She stood, turned her back on him, and left without another word, but under her breath, she mumbled, "You'll see, Simon Gilby. I'll match your game. Someday I'll be as rich as you. I don't need you for anything."

She remembered the book she'd liked so much that she'd just finished reading and smiled evilly. "The Count of Monte Cristo had the right idea, Simon Gilby. Revenge will be sweet."

Tom was crushed by Meredith's desertion, but even he had to admit that there were noticeable advantages to her being gone. As soon as she left, Tom's work improved. It was the only solace he had, and he threw himself into the affairs of Lowell and Hughes as if his life depended on it. Everyone in the family approved of the change in him, and Granddad even hinted of a promotion in the firm if he kept up the good work.

By the time Meredith had been gone a month he was exhausted, and Tom retreated to his apartment to spend a weekend alone. It was the last weekend he'd have in the home he and Meredith had shared. Without her financial assistance, there was no way he could keep the place. He wasn't sorry to be leaving it; all it held were memories of her.

Tom spent all day on Saturday packing his belongings, and by Sunday morning the place looked more like a storage closet than a home. The sight of all the boxes began to depress him, and he decided to take a good brisk hike in the park, hoping that would perk him up.

The park was full of children playing in the snow. Tom stopped to watch some of them busily building a snowman. He smiled at their efforts and the intense concentration they were devoting to the project. Finally he moved on toward a pond full of ice skaters. One in particular caught his attention. Her bright red hair was unmistakable. It was Carol.

"Carol!" he shouted, glad to see a familiar face.

She turned and dug a skate tip into the ice, stopping instantly. When she saw who it was she glided toward him. "Tom, how wonderful to see you. It's been too long."

She was breathing hard from the exercise, and her cheeks were pink with the cold. Her hair shone in the sun. Looking at Carol now, full of vitality and joy, Tom wondered how he ever could have thought Meredith was so beautiful.

Carol threw her multi-colored striped scarf around her neck and joined him on the bench beside the frozen pond. "Glorious day, isn't it?"

"Now it is," Tom said, feeling for the first time that there was hope for the future.

Chapter Seven

Sons and Lovers

"Mom, I don't know what I would have done if you hadn't let me move in with you." Tom said, as he dumped the last of his things onto the living-room floor. Lisa looked askance at the mess and then decided to ignore it for the moment. "You know I'm strapped. I spent every nickel I had."

Lisa went over to Tom and hugged him. "That's what mothers are for. I know how you feel," she told him, thinking of the way Simon teated her. "You don't have to be young to be foolish, you know."

"I guess Simon did the same thing to you as Meredith did to me, "Tom said in sympathy.

"How're you holding up?" Lisa asked, trying to get him off the subject.

"I'm just fine, Mom. Carol's been great."

"Carol?" Lisa inquired. "Are you seeing her again?"

Tom grinned. "Sure am. Why didn't you clobber me with something when I dropped her for Meredith? I sure deserved it."

"Would you have listened?"

"Guess not. I suppose I had to learn the hard way."

"We all do. I'm glad you and Carol have mended things. She's really a lovely girl."

And you, Mom?"

"I'm a survivor, hasn't anyone ever told you that? As a matter of fact, I'm just getting ready to go out."

"I'm glad," Tom said as he appraised her. Lisa's hair was pinned up, and she was wearing a champagne colored suit. "By the way, Mom. You look terrific."

"Why thank you, sir," she replied, thinking how much like his father he was. "You're quite the gentleman."

"Yours is not the only negative report. Rick Ryan just isn't performing well enough," Dr. Nelson, Director of Residents, said, handing Bob a folder. "I thought you could speak to him. See what the problem is. Maybe you can straighten him out."

Bob hesitated, thinking about the tension between Rick and him. "I'm not sure I'm the one to—"

"He is your wife's son, I believe."

Jennifer walked in just as Dr. Nelson had mentioned her. She nodded to Dr. Nelson and looked questioningly at Bob. "Bob?" she said, wondering what was going on.

"It's your son," Dr. Nelson said. "His performance is simply not up to par. I'll leave this with you, Bob," he said walking toward the door.

Bob briefly looked over the report and grimaced. "It's not good, Jenny. He's really screwing up."

"Talk to him, Bob. Maybe he'll straighten up if you tell him how bad it is. His father was so proud of him. I'd hate to see him ruin his future."

"Jenny, I can't," Bob said, putting the records aside.

"But Bob, there's no one else to turn to."

"Do you think he'd listen to me? He avoids me as if I poison the atmosphere by my mere presence."

"You're exaggerating," Jennifer said. "Why, I think things have gotten better between the two of you."

"You're not being honest with yourself, Jenny. You want them to be better so much, you just won't see what's really going on. If anything, it's worse than ever. I'm not the one to handle this problem. But I think *you* should."

Jennifer took Rick's records off the desk and looked them over. "Bob, what's this?" She handed him one of the evaluation papers, the one he had written.

It hadn't been easy to write what he'd really believed. In fact, he'd tried to downplay some of the more serious problems, but Rick had changed an order Bob had made on a chart and had jeopardized a patient's well being. That was unforgivable.

"I can't believe he'd do anything like this," Jennifer said in astonishment.

"Nevertheless, Jenny, he was most definitely responsible."

"But why would he do such a thing?"

Bob didn't want to hurt her but he felt it best to be honest. "Possibly, to make me look bad."

Jennifer looked as if he'd hit her. "You can't believe that, Bob! He's my son! You know how he's hurting right now. You could have been easier on him."

"And I'm your husband," Bob said. "Would you have me lie to protect him?"

Tears she could no longer hold back, streamed down Jennifer's cheeks. She had to see Rick, to try to better the situation, but by choosing to help her son, was she turning her back on Bob?

Lisa was meeting Victor Ulich at The Rib, a barbecue place on Mainstreet. She'd been introduced to Victor by a friend and when he'd asked her out for the third time, she convinced herself it was time to stop looking back and get on with life. Finally, she accepted his invitation to dinner. She watched Victor come through the door and look around for her. He was a far cry from the suave and elegant Simon. Overweight and mostly bald, he looked like an aging shoe salesman at the local mall. Lisa tried to smile as he approached.

"Have you been waiting long?"

"Oh, no," she said. "Just a minute or two."

He took her hand and didn"t let go. "Good."

She didn't know why she had the urge to pull away and leave. She resisted it and followed the hostess to a table. They both ordered the Friday night special which had made The Rib such a popular spot: baby back ribs, cole slaw, baked potatoes, and cinnamon coffee.

"We'll have dessert later," Victor said, leering at her.

Not another one, Lisa thought with disgust. *How do I get myself into these situations?*

She looked at Victor, sitting across from her in the booth, gnawing at his ribs, and wished he'd disappear. But his unpleasant image remained solidly before her.

When dinner was over, Victor slid his bulk across the booth and wrapped his arm around her. Lisa felt as if she was being smothered. Still trying to be polite, she tried to wriggle away, but he kept his greasy hands on her leg.

"Let's go," he said, just about drooling with anticipation.

"No," Lisa replied, trying to delay being alone with him. "I'd like another cup of coffee, please." She waved at the waitress to get her attention and a reprieve. As she sipped the coffee, Victor nudged his leg up against her thigh in a suggestive gesture.

Lisa jerked away, spilling the coffee on her suit.

"Now see what you've made me do."

"Need help?" Came the familiar and welcome voice of Donald Hughes.

"Do I!" Lisa said gratefully.

"Guess you'll need a ride home to change," Donald said, indicating the spill, and picking up on her distress.

"Oh, yes," Lisa said eagerly. "Must get this coffee cleaned off before my suit is ruined. You don't mind, do you Victor? Donald lives right near me and I don't want to take you out of your way. Thanks for dinner. It was very nice." She hopped out of the booth and tore out of the restaurant with Donald before Victor had a chance to protest.

"I guess I do believe in knights on chargers after all," Lisa said when they were safely in the car.

Donald laughed. "Even if the knight's got a 400 horsepower white Cadillac instead of a romantic trusty white steed, Lisa?"

"The more horses the better. I can't get away from that sleazy character fast enough."

"Where'd you find him?" Donald asked with amusement.

"Don't tease me, Donald. Just let me be the grateful damsel you've rescued. Okay?"

"Okay," he said, and they both laughed with relief.

* * *

Jennifer saw Rick enter the hospital cafeteria with John Dixon. They seemed to be friends and she wondered how long they'd been so chummy. She'd arranged to meet Rick for lunch and waited for him to join her while John sat at another table.

She hadn't had a chance to be with Rick for over a month and noticed he'd lost weight. "Are you sure you're all right?" she asked with motherly concern.

"Mom, I'm a resident. We never sleep. Remember? Just a few more months and I'll be out of this grind."

"That's what I wanted to talk to you about, Rick. You're not doing very well."

"Who told you that?" Rick demanded. "No, don't tell me, the grand and glorious Doctor Bob, I'll bet. John warned me he would."

"I wouldn't put my entire faith in John Dixon," Jennifer warned. "He has a way of exaggerating, I think."

"Another of Bob's sage observations?" Rick asked.

"Rick," she said sternly. "That's enough. Bob is as concerned about your situation as I am. He's the one who asked me to talk to you."

Rick threw down his fork and got up to leave. "In that case, Mother, maybe we'd just better call the whole thing off."

Jennifer grabbed his arm. "Rick Ryan. You're going to explain what's going on. Your father was so proud of you, and just look what you're doing. You may never get your resident's credentials."

"You leave Dad out of this," Rick said angrily. "His memory is only a convenience for you to use when you want something from me."

Jennifer almost slapped her son right then and there.

"Rick, can't you see how much you're hurting all of us."

"What did the saintly doctor tell you about me, Mother?"

"That you changed an order on a chart and risked a patient's life."

"And you believed him. You didn't ask me about what happened. You just took his word."

"I'm here, with you, aren't I? Tell me, Rick. What really happened? Can't you see I'm trying to understand your point of view?" she pleaded.

"He wrote an order and it was wrong so he blamed me. Residents make good scapegoats, Mother. He was trying to get rid of me."

"I can't believe—"

"You won't believe me. You don't really want to."

Rick stalked out of the cafeteria, leaving Jennifer staring after him.

"Donald," Nancy said, astonished at his news. "Lisa? You can't be serious."

"Why not, Mom? She's changed. You really should give her a chance."

"Lisa, change? I doubt it very much, Donald. I feel sorry for her. She has no one and I'm sure she's very lonely, but you know what misery Bob went through with her."

"That was years ago," Donald said, swiping a freshly baked chocolate chip cookie from the counter where it had been cooling.

"Donald, you'll spoil your dinner."

"And your life," Chris said, entering the room. "Lisa's trouble, Donald. Don't get serious about her."

Donald laughed. "You'd think I was going to marry

her tomorrow. We enjoy each other's company. What's wrong with friendship?"

"Lisa doesn't know anything about friendship," Nancy warned. "She only knows marriage and she has a tendency to be predatory about it."

Bob, joined them in the kitchen. "What's this about Lisa?"

"Not you too?" Donald said. "Mom and Dad were just warning me about her."

"Well, she is a handful, Don. Nobody knows better than I. Remember that."

"I hope you all won't pounce on her. She's going to be here for dinner any minute."

"Pounce?" Nancy asked. "Of course we won't pounce. We just don't want to see you hurt, that's all."

"I think you'll all be sorry you've misjudged her so badly," Donald said as the doorbell rang. "She's really made an effort to change. Why she even reads Shakespeare now."

"Shakespeare?" Bob said with disbelief. "That I've got to see to believe."

Much to the delight of the entire Hughes clan, Tom and Carol began seeing each other regularly again. The girl seemed to make a great difference in Tom. He became more cheerful, and his work at the law office was exemplary once more.

Carol and Tom were lying in front of the fireplace in Lisa's apartment, his head on her lap. Tom smiled contentedly, his eyes were closed, and he felt warm and happy.

"If I could purr, I would," Tom said, luxuriating in the feel of her hand stroking his thick brown hair. "You know, Carol, we've been seeing each other every night for weeks, and it's been great. The hardest part of my day is when I have to take you home."

"I don't like to leave you either," she said softly. "I could stay like this forever."

Tom looked up into her eyes. He took her hand in his and slowly brought it to his lips. After what seemed to Carol like a moment of indecision he got up and went into his room. A moment later he reappeared and sat crossed legged in front of her. "I thought it might be too soon for this, but I just can't wait. We belong together."

Carol's heart pounded as Tom took a small velvet box from his pocket. He opened it, took out a shining object, and held it up for her to see.

"Tom, it's beautiful!" Carol exclaimed. "And it could never be too soon. I love you so much it hurts. I think I've always loved you, even when I was a little girl."

Her hand trembled slightly as he slipped the ring onto her finger.

An ardent kiss sealed their troth.

Carol held her hand out toward the firelight, so she could admire the ring. The diamond was rose colored, pear shaped, and set in pink gold. On the larger end of the diamond, five good sized rubies formed a curved base. The stones gleamed brightly in the firelight.

"It's beautiful, and so unusual." She kissed him again.

"It's warm, like you are, and the rubies remind me of your hair." He tenderly touched the end of one of the stray red strands. "It's you, Carol, warm, beautiful, glowing . . . "

"I love it, Tom, and I love you. But how could you possibly have afforded it?"

"You don't ever have to worry about such things," he

said, holding her close "I've got very good prospects, in case you haven't noticed."

"If I haven't noticed my family certainly has," she said lightly. She stood up, her hands on her hips, and deepening her voice, imitated her father. "Carol Deming. That Hughes fella is a very good catch, ya know. You've been out with him a lot lately. Think he's ever gonna pop the question. We're not gettin' any younger, girl. It's time for a grandchild or two." She dissolved into laughter and hugged Tom playfully.

"We'll have lots of kids," Tom told her, laughing almost as much as she was. "All girls, and all the image of their mother."

Just at that moment Lisa and Donald came through the door. Lisa bustled across the room to Carol and Tom. "We wanted to be the first to congratulate you two."

Carol was taken aback. How could anyone possibly know about their engagement? As Lisa kissed her on the cheek, Carol suddenly figured it out. Then she realized how. The ring. That's how Tom could afford it. Lisa must have helped him out. Somehow it made her feel a little uncomfortable.

"I have a little something in the way of an engagement present," Lisa said, hardly allowing time for Carol to respond. She handed the girl a small box.

Speechless, Carol looked to Tom, then to Lisa and Donald.

"Well, aren't you going to open it?" Lisa asked.

Tom's mother reminded Carol of a little girl at a birthday party. She was a far cry from her own parents who were constantly pressed for cash.

"Go ahead, Carol," Tom said, "before Mom

dies of anticipation."

"All right." Carol, a little embarrassed by all the attention, struggled with the bow, then opened the box. In her hand she held a small music box, decorated with porceline figures of a shepherd and shepherdess, embracing in a garland of pastel colored china flowers. She opened the box and it tinkled out the tune of "Love is a Many Splendored Thing".

"It's lovely," Carol said, kissing Lisa on the cheek. "Thank you. I'll always treasure it."

Tom kissed Lisa also. "Thanks, Mom, for everything," Tom said, kissing his mother.

Donald offered his hand to Tom in congratulations, while Lisa chattered enthusiastically. "You know how mushy I get about love," she said, as a tear trickled down her cheek. "Carol, we'll have to get right on with the wedding plans. I just love weddings."

Bob suspected that John Dixon and Rick Ryan were joining forces against him. Rick was attached to the cardiac unit and had ample opportunity to be in John's company. The growing friendship between the two men concerned Bob greatly, but there wasn't anything he could do about it.

More distressing still, Bob had noticed a puzzling change in Jennifer ever since her meeting with Rick. Refusing to talk about her son or what they had discussed, she seemed distant and unapproachable.

What did Rick say to her? Bob wondered. Things were not going well, and Bob felt helpless to change them.

He was meeting Jennifer for lunch at the hospital in hopes of making a stab at some better communication. She was waiting in the lobby of the Inn for him when he arrived, looking as lovely as ever, but definitely not her old cheerful self.

"I invited Kim to join us," Jennifer said as she watched her sister walk across the lobby from the rest room.

"I wanted to talk alone," Bob muttered under his breath, but he smiled when Kim joined them. No use getting her involved in their problems.

Since the luncheon was not going to accomplish Bob's primary goal of achieving some better communication with his wife, he decided to make the best of it. He always liked Kim's company, and with his work at the hospital having been so demanding of late, he hadn't had much of a chance to see her. He still hardly knew anything about Jennifer's sister.

Kim added cheer to what would have been a difficult situation for Bob. She chatted lightly about Oakdale and its people, about how much she liked the small-town atmosphere, and about the possibility of remaining there.

"You're seriously considering settling here?" Bob asked, surprised and disturbed by the excitement he felt at the prospect.

"Why, yes. Jennifer's my only family and I have no ties anywhere else. I'm sure this is a wonderful place to settle."

"Take my word for it," John Dixon said, coming up behind Bob. "This town has a lot to offer. It's provincial in some ways, but Chicago isn't too far away. I'd be happy to show you some of the more interesting spots in town, what there is of them, that is."

Kim looked up at the stranger, wondering about his audacity. Then she glanced at Bob for an explanation.

From his expression she could tell her brother-in-law was not at all pleased with the intrusion. Or perhaps, she thought after briefly evaluating the situation, it was the intruder he was taking exception to.

"Aren't you going to introduce me, Bob?" John asked cheerily, taking the extra seat at the table. He looked at Bob, who had turned a bright shade of red and moved the chair closer to the table. "In that case, I'll introduce myself. Dr. John Dixon."

"John, this is my sister, Kim Reynolds," Jennifer said, before Bob could say what was on his mind.

"Very pleased to meet you, Kim. Mind if I join you?" John picked up a menu. "I thought this meal was going to be dull. Now just see how wrong I was."

He glanced coldly at Bob, then turned his attention to Kim.

At first Lisa thought Donald and Bob were very much alike, but the more time she spent with Donald, the more obvious the differences became. Donald had suggested a weekend away from Oakdale and small-town scrutiny, and Lisa had jumped at the chance to get away. The weather had cleared, but it was bitterly cold when they headed for Chicago. The drive wasn't long and they arrived at their hotel in time for a late dinner.

Much to Lisa's delight, Donald, unlike Bob, didn't seem to worry much about money. He'd rented an extravagant suite for them, and their dinner in the penthouse restaurant of the hotel was elegant and costly.

Lisa loved the chance to show off her latest gown from Paris. It was teal blue lace over a natural shell, and it gave an enticing suggestion of nudity beneath the lace. She could tell by Donald's stares, it wasn't lost on him.

Getting out of Oakdale gave them both a chance to throw off any inhibitions they might have felt before. Donald seemed a different person here, much more relaxed, joking, and full of fun, and Lisa had an opportunity to let loose and planned on taking every advantage of it.

After dinner she stood looking out at the lights of the city. Donald came up behind her and put his arm about her waist. "It's beautiful," Lisa said. "Like all the lights are little twinking stars below us and we're up here in heaven."

"That's where you belong, Lisa. Up in the stars. Your hair is the sun, you know, and I'm being blinded by your light."

"Why Donald, I didn't know you were a poet," she said, turning to him.

"I didn't either," he answered with amusement. "I guess it's this place and you."

"You do have a way of making me feel very special. You know how much I need you, Donald. I was so desolate . . ."

"You've done the same for me, Lisa." He took her in his arms and felt her heart race.

The blue lace gown soon lay on the floor, and Lisa lay on the bed wearing only the natural colored satin underdress.

"You're driving me wild," he said, reaching for her.

Lisa wiggled away and let the top of the dress slip down, teasing him all the more.

Through the window, the moon set over a sleeping city as the two made love with uninhibited passion.

Chapter Eight
The Wedding of the Year

Nancy Hughes stood beside Chris, watching the wedding guests enter the church. The grandparents of the groom were beaming with pride and happiness.

Lisa sat conspicuously by herself in a pew behind the elder members of the Hughes family. Bob was serving as Tom's best man, and was busy with the groom, and Donald was serving as an usher and would join her later.

As usual, Lisa looked spectacular. Knowing Carol had chosen fall colors for the wedding, she was wearing a copper colored shimmering gown which had been made in Chicago especially for the occasion. A matching topaz necklace, bracelet and earrings in dull gold antique settings completed her outfit.

The church looked beautiful. Sprays, of peach and white gladiolas were attached to the pews with bronze ribbon, and the flowers on the altar, in shades of peach and orange and red, were gorgeous. Amber colored candles, each with a peachy bow, gave a warm glow to the altar.

This was the church where Lisa and Bob had been married, and the memories kept intruding on her happiness for her son. *I hope they're happier than we were*, she wished. *They have to be. Carol has much more sense than I had at that age.* Lisa didn't know of one person who didn't like Carol. Sadly, she couldn't say the same for herself, but then nobody could ever say that Lisa Shea was dull.

The guests were all seated and the church was packed. Donald, having completed his usher's duties joined her just as the music booming from the church organ quieted everyone down. All turned to see the groom come down the aisle.

Tom looked wonderful in his gray morning suit. And his peach ascot made his brown hair seem darker than it really was. The father looked as wonderful as the son, Lisa thought, and another twinge of regret went through her. She put her hand on Donald's elbow for comfort and he, thinking she was feeling a mother's natural regret at losing her son, took her hand and smiled to comfort her. Jennifer and Kim had joined the elder members of the Hughes family in the pew in front of them, making Lisa feel all the more left out of the immediate family.

The music softened and the maid of honor walked down the aisle. She was wearing a simple gown of peach silk, and was carrying a small bouquet of two-tone sweetheart roses.

The Wedding March began and everyone waited anxiously for the bride to make her appearance.

Carol walked down the aisle on her father's arm. Mr. Deming, a lanky man, tanned from his days in the fields, looking nervous and out of place, walked stiff legged beside his beautiful daughter. His eyes darted from one side of the church to the other. He looked as if he were searching for a way to escape, and Lisa felt a tinge of sympathy for him.

Lisa had to admit that Carol made a spectacular bride. Carol had always possessed a pretty, wholesome look which Lisa never imagined could have been transformed into such a sophisticated loveliness. She seemed to glow in her classic satin antique-white gown. A long veil, attached to a coronet of apricot roses, flowed over her red hair. Even with the veil lowered, Lisa could see the happiness on Carol's face as she passed her.

Carol's father put his daughter's hand gently into Tom's, then gratefully eased into the background as Reverend White stepped forward.

Carol and Tom stood side by side, gazing lovingly into each others eyes, as the reverend recited the vows. Tom's deep voice filled the church as he repeated them, and Carol's soft voice hardly carried past the first few rows. The couple exchanged rings and the bride and groom kissed. The kiss lasted a great deal longer than usual, and everyone in the church was delighted.

Seldom had Oakdale seen such an attractive and happy couple.

Anyone who was anybody in Oakdale was invited to the reception. It was the social event of the year, held at the Oakdale Inn's Regent Ballroom.

Everyone assembled around the wedding cake, a tower of a confection, decorated with real flowers. Carol had taken off her veil. Her classic gown and her red hair gave her the look of an elegant renaissance lady.

After the bride and groom had cut the cake, Bob and Lisa circulated and the Demings greeted their guests. Bob and his parents were quick to notice how closely Donald attended Lisa. Although they all disapproved of their relationship, they knew this was not the time to make an issue of it. Everything they could say had been said many times, to no effect. It worried Nancy. But there was another problem which concerned her even more.

"Chris," Nancy said, "have you noticed something peculiar going on tonight?"

Chris looked puzzled. "Everything seems to have gone off like clockwork. I've never seen two happier young people."

"It's not Tom and Carol I'm concerned about," Nancy said seriously. "It's Bob and Jennifer. They haven't said more than two words to each other all evening."

"Bob's been so busy with being best man and host here—"

"No," Nancy said, frowning worriedly. "I don't understand what it is, but there's something more."

When Kim arrived at the reception with John Dixon, Bob was astonished and not at all pleased. Kim looked lovely, and he was disturbed that he was so intensely aware of her. He did his best to be pleasant and went over to greet them. "I hope you're enjoying the reception."

"Enjoying it!" John said enthusiastically. "It's great. Everyone who matters is here. I've had a chance to meet and talk to the chairman of the hospital board, the editor of the Oakdale Press, and the chief of police. I've even been invited to join the Oakdale Country

Club. And this sister-in-law of yours," he held Kim closer. "Wow! She's a knockout!"

Bob groaned when Kim grinned and held John's hand tighter.

All evening Bob watched John with Kim, until finally, he couldn't restrain himself any longer. He discreetly took Kim aside. "I hate to interfere with your life, Kim," he said. "I know it's really none of my business, but I feel John Dixon is really not to be trusted."

Kim smiled. "In what way, Bob?"

"That's just it. I don't really know. It's just a very uncomfortable feeling I have about him."

"Jennifer's told me about your disagreements at Memorial. It's not unusual, I'm told, for doctors to disagree."

"It's not that, Kim. I've disagreed with colleagues before. There's something different about him. Be careful. I have a feeling he sees you as a rung up the social ladder and might take advantage . . ."

Donald had planned on dropping Lisa off and then going home, but realizing that she really wanted his company, he decided to stay the night.

"Why don't you take a hot bath while I fix something to drink? You look as if you're about to unspring any moment. Do you miss Tom that much already?"

"I guess so," she said, not wanting to share her true feelings with him. She went into the bathroom and stripped for her bath, thinking of her plans for the future. The more she saw of Bob, the more she wanted him. She certainly couldn't let anyone know that. Especially since Bob was happily married and there simply wasn't any way Lisa could see of making her dreams to remarry him come true.

On the other hand, she had decided she really liked Donald and was set on capturing him instead. *He* was available—and he was a Hughes too. She couldn't help but compare the brothers. Bob was dark, assured, always the competent physician. Donald took after his father, had lighter hair and was bigger boned than his brother, and had chosen to follow his father in the law. Upon examination, Lisa thought Donald came off a good second best. The bath water was getting cold. Lisa wrapped herself in a towel and when dry, put on a spectacular red silk kimono. Donald was standing at the window when she sauntered into the living room, her robe shimmering in the dim light.

"You're so special, Donald Hughes. How did I ever live without you?" she said, trying to sound convincing.

Donald turned and smiled. "You managed very well, if I can refresh your memory, Lisa. You married twice since you divorced Bob, and each time managed to come out ahead. You're a far cry from that little schoolgirl he married. As a matter of fact, I think the mother of the groom looked spectacular tonight."

"So did the groom's uncle. I think we made a very good looking pair."

Donald had changed into a robe that he kept at her place. Now he disappeared into the kitchen and returned with two glasses of warm milk laced with rum.

Lisa, her hair piled on her head, joined him on the couch. "This is wonderful. It's just what I needed."

He handed her a glass and she sipped it slowly. "Mmmm, luscious, and so relaxing. You do have a calming effect on me, Donald Hughes." She put the glass down on the table, rested her head on his shoulder and in a few minutes was asleep. Donald lifted Lisa into his arms and carried her into the bedroom, gently placing her on the bed. Lisa sighed in her sleep and nestled into the pillow. He placed the coverlet over her, turned off the light, and climbed in beside her.

Lisa had a huge breakfast prepared before Donald awoke. He groaned when she kissed him, then opened his eyes and smiled up at her.

"Good morning, sleepyhead," she said. "Breakfast is ready."

"So early?" Donald asked, rolling over.

"Donald Hughes, it's half past eleven . . ."

He jumped out of bed. "Why didn't you get me up sooner? I'm late." He began dressing quickly, then realized it was too late to worry about sleeping through the morning. "Guess I'll make it into the office this afternoon."

"I'll bet there's not one member of the Hughes family that makes it into the office this morning," Lisa said jokingly. "Come on, get ready. Your breakfast is getting cold."

"I'm going to have to go home to change. Can't go to the office in a tux . . ."

"Well, I told you to leave an extra change of clothes here, but you're so stubborn."

"I didn't think it was appropriate."

"Isn't it a bit late for that, Donald? It's not as if everyone doesn't know we're seeing each other."

"We've got to talk about that, Lisa."

"I thought you'd get around to it sooner or later. It'll be so much less of a problem when we marry. Why, then, no one could object to our relationship. I just knew you'd be coming to that conclusion soon yourself. Oh, Donald, we'll be so happy."

He looked stricken. The blood drained from his face. "Lisa. What ever gave you the idea we would get married?"

"Why you, of course. You've been so attentive. I thought . . ."

Donald could see happiness had turned to distress, Lisa's animation to a strange embarrassed quiet.

"You never had any intention of marrying me," she pouted, staring down at the floor.

"I never said I did. We have fun together. I enjoy your company a great deal. But marriage, Lisa? Can you honestly say you love me?"

"Of course I can," she insisted with a hint of annoyance.

"Honestly, Lisa? I know you like me, and you depend on me. Maybe that's a kind of love, but it's not the kind that sustains a relationship."

"But I thought you loved me."

"I do, in a way. I love the fun in you. I love your energy, and I love being your lover. You're quite a woman."

"But not quite enough to be your wife, is that it? The Hughes family has won again, haven't they? They never did like me," she said petulantly.

"This has nothing to do with Mother and Dad—or Bob. They've voiced their objections, but they have nothing to do with this, Lisa. This is between you and me. I had no idea you wanted such a commitment. Under the circumstances, I think we should stop seeing each other."

"But Donald . . ."

He left without saying goodbye.

Lisa sank onto the sofa, overcome by a desperate feeling. "There's just got to be something I can do to change his mind," she told herself. She had to get her Hughes!

When Carol and Tom arrived at the honeymoon suite at their hotel in San Francisco, a bouquet of apricot roses, a box of Swiss chocolates, and a bottle of cooled vintage champagne awaited them. The note on the bottle read:

> From your loving grandparents,
> Many happy years.

"That was sweet of them," Carol said. "Your family has been absolutely wonderful to me, Tom."

"That's because they love you almost as much as I do," he replied, popping the cork on the champagne. He filled two long-stemmed crystal glasses and they locked arms, for the first sip. "To you, Mrs. Hughes," Tom toasted her.

"Mrs. Hughes. That sounds so wonderful." Carol put down her glass and kissed him.

"Tired?" Tom asked, rubbing Carol's shoulders.

"Exhausted, but I want this night to go on forever."

"It will," Tom assured her. "Our marriage will be a perpetual honeymoon. I promise."

Carol changed into the white satin nightgown Lisa had given her and joined Tom in the bedroom. He watched her come from the bathroom, fresh and beaming, a lovely vision. He took her hand and led her to the bed. Theirs had been an innocent love, awaiting this bridal night for consummation. Tom could feel Carol's tension; he kissed her gently before joining her in the king sized bed. The satin of Carol's gown enhanced the silkiness and glow of her fair skin. Tom ran his hand over both, gently stripping the gown off her soft body.

Carol sighed, and ran her hand down his chest, sending shivers of pleasure through him. It was all Tom could do to hold back the passion within him, but he forced himself to be calm.

She arched to his touch as he ran his hand down her neck and followed the curve of her body. "Oh, Tom," she moaned.

He whispered into her ear, all those endearments he knew she needed to assure her. He was not a novice lover and he wanted this night to be perfect for her. There would be no rushing tonight. He wanted nothing to spoil their ultimate moment together.

Carol held Tom close, wanting him more than she'd ever wanted anything before. His hair smelled spicy and wonderful, and his touch was electrifying. His hands were gentle, finding those places which made her almost cry with pleasure.

His caresses became more demanding, and her body responded with a desire that matched his own. Finally they were united by their love for each other. A few moments later, they fell asleep to the deep wailing sound of the distant foghorns.

Lisa had not been seen for days. She'd stayed in her apartment, trying vainly to come up with a plan to convince Donald to change his mind. Nothing seemed appropriate so she'd been sulking alone. Beside being desolate about her breakup with Donald, she had a touch of stomach flu and felt absolutely miserable.

When the phone rang, she considered not answering it, but the caller was so persistent that she finally did.

It was Nancy Hughes. "Lisa?"

Surprised, Lisa studied the phone, before saying anything.

"Lisa, are you all right?"

"Just a touch of the flu," Lisa answered in a monotone.

"When we hadn't heard anything from you, we were worried."

"Why? I'm perfectly able to get along."

"Donald told us he isn't seeing you anymore. He was concerned . . ."

"I see," Lisa said. "And you thought I'd be distraught?"

"It did occur to us."

"Don't worry about me. I'm a survivor, remember?"

"You don't sound at all like yourself."

"It's the flu. I'm sure I'll be fine in a day or so."

"Have you seen a doctor?"

"Over a little upset stomach? Of course not. I'll just stay warm and cozy and it'll pass."

"I'll send Donald over with something."

Nancy just had to be always mothering someone, Lisa thought. "No! Please, Nancy. I'll be fine. Really."

After she'd hung up, Lisa thought that Nancy had not sounded terribly convinced, but at least Donald wasn't coming over. Lisa walked to the kitchen, heated a cup of tea and put some honey and brandy into it. She never remembered feeling quite so queasy and thought the brew would help settle her stomach. As the day progressed she felt much better and began to perk up. She went to bed feeling considerably better and vowed to go out the next day.

"I'll show them I'm all right," she said. "Imagine thinking I'd pine away for Donald."

The next morning she felt worse than ever, and even lost her light breakfast. Then she had a disturbing realization. She checked her calendar. "My God, six weeks! I'm two complete weeks late!" she said aloud. "Better in the evening, sick in the morning. I couldn't be. Or could I?" What if she was pregnant. A baby was the last thing she wanted or needed at this stage in her life.

When she had finally gotten control of herself, Lisa wondered what she should do. *I can't have a baby,* she thought *I'll have to have an abortion. But Donald doesn't have to know I've made that decision until after we're married.*

She decided to wait one week before telling him she was pregnant. Tom and Carol would be back then and she could share the news of her marriage to Donald with everyone. She had no doubt he'd do the right thing. After all, he was a Hughes. Everyone in the Hughes family always did the right thing!

The fog burned off by mid morning, and the San Francisco day became sunny and cool. Carol and Tom left the hotel around eleven o'clock, just as the sun hit the bay, turning it into a sparkling backdrop for the city.

They headed to Chinatown, stopping to watch a mime in Union Square on the way. Chinatown was a bustle of people. The smells of fried noodles, poultry, fish, and unusual spices made the city seem exotic to the two midwesterners.

"Look, Tom," Carol said, pointing to the roast ducks hanging in the window of one of the restaurants. "They still have their heads on."

"They're supposed to be a real delicacy. Want to try one?"

Carol looked tentative. "Okay, I guess. So long as it isn't staring up at me when they serve it."

Carol's first priority was purchasing gifts for everyone. After they ate, they explored some of San Francisco's many boutiques. While Carol shopped, Tom browsed. She was so busy with making her choices she didn't see him purchase a gift for her.

That evening they had dinner at the restaurant on top of the Hyatt Regency. The revolving restaurant constantly turned, offering a spectacular view of the city and bay. When they sat down they were facing the water; the Bay Bridge's span was lit brightly, spanning the bay, it looked like two towers of light floating unattached above the water in the fog.

After a meal of fresh crab and salad, Tom ordered after-dinner drinks and gave his gift to Carol.

"Tom? What's this?" she asked in genuine surprise.

"For you, of course. I couldn't resist buying them."

She opened the case and pulled out a strand of perfectly matched pink pearls. "They're beautiful!" she exclaimed. "Oh, Tom, you shouldn't have."

He stood and clasped the necklace around her neck. The warm pink of the pearls matched her blush. "They're even more beautiful when they're on you," he said, brushing her neck with his lips. "You bring out their true luster and color."

That night they walked back to their hotel, lost in each other and the gray mist of the bay.

Chapter Nine
Devastated Love

Rick Ryan surreptitiously made his way down the corridor to C.C.U. He glanced around every few steps to make sure no one would see him entering the area. He ducked behind a wall into another corridor when a nurse went by, and waited for her to go back to the nurse's station, before he continued. He made it to the medicine room without being noticed and breathed a sigh of relief before he picked up the phone and dialed the C.C.U. nurses's station.

"Mrs. Helstrom," he said, in a deepened, disguised voice. "Would you please check the window in the east corridor."

"I'm alone here at the moment," she said. "I'll check it as soon as I can."

Rick pounded a fist into the desk. He just had to get her away from her station. "Maintenance requires a check immediately. If there's a cold draft we may be forced to remove the patients from that wing. Don't make the situation worse by ignoring orders!"

Mrs. Helstrom, an old-timer at Memorial, looked

around worriedly. It wasn't proper to leave her station, but the removal of patients was serious.

Rick had made sure the window in the east wing was broken. He'd done it himself earlier. The window faced north and the cold wind was blowing through the area. Mrs. Helstrom would have something real to report. In the meantime, she would be heading to the farthest place on the floor, away from the C.C.U.

From the barely open door of the medicine room, Rick watched the nurse walk down the hall toward the east wing. It was four A.M., the time he knew the other nurse on duty took a break. He'd been planning this night for quite some time and had considered everything carefully.

Bob's patient, Mr. Greeley, was in the glass partitioned area directly in front of the nurses's station. The young doctor quickly walked across the hall and into the C.C.U. patient area. The only noise in the room was the labored breathing of the old man, and the sound of a respirator. Rick glanced at the patient. He was almost dead, clinging to life by the grace of machinery and Bob Hughes' tenaciousness.

"This time I won't get caught," Rick said under his breath, as he entered the monitoring room. He was holding Mr. Greeley's chart when Mrs. Helstrom surprised him. She was a big woman, who looked as if she could single-handedly lift a patient, bed and all. "What are you doing here?" she asked brusquely.

"Checking this chart," Rick said as his heart jumped into his throat.

"By what authority?"

"Dr. Hughes."

"He said nothing to me about a resident being

assigned to this case. Say, you're Rick Ryan, aren't you? You're not on this service anymore."

"I've been following this case," Rick said lamely.

Mrs. Helstrom was no fool. "At four o'clock in the morning, Doctor?"

"Okay, I'll leave," Rick said, heading quickly out the door.

"Wait a minute," the wary nurse said. "Hey! Stop!" she called after him, but it was too late. He was on his way down the stairs.

Bob answered the phone wearily.

"Dr. Hughes, this is Inga Helstrom."

"Yes, Inga," he said, suddenly wide awake. "Mr. Greeley?"

"No, doctor, something odd just occurred. I wanted to check it out with you."

"Odd?" Bob asked. "What?"

"Did you ask Dr. Ryan to check in on Mr. Greeley?" Bob was fully alert now. "Why?"

Jennifer had awakened and had turned on the light. "What's wrong?" she asked, but Bob didn't answer.

"He was just here in C.C.U., Doctor, and was looking at Mr. Greeley's chart. The door between the monitoring room and the patient area was open. I didn't leave it that way before I was called away—"

"Called away? Have you checked on Mr. Greeley?"

"His signs are all the same, Doctor. Everything is monitoring as stable."

"Check him again carefully. I'm on my way, and Inga, lock his chart in the medicine closet, please."

"The medicine closet?"

"Just do as I say. I'll be there in a few minutes."

* * *

Against his better judgment, Donald found himself standing in front of Lisa's door. She'd sounded so distressed, he felt he couldn't ignore her plea to come over, particularly when Nancy told him she'd been ill. When Lisa answered the door he was glad he'd come. For once, she hadn't been exaggerating. She really did look ill.

Lisa sank into the couch and Donald took a chair opposite her. "Mom told me you weren't well. Have you seen a doctor?"

"I don't need a doctor, Donald."

"Stubborn as usual," Donald said. "I insist—"

"It's not the flu."

"Since when did you become a doctor, Lisa?"

"It doesn't take a doctor to know what's wrong with me, Donald." She paused for a long, dramatic moment. "I'm pregnant!"

Donald was dumbstruck. "Are you sure?"

"I'm three weeks late and sick in the mornings. In fact, I'm sick most of the day. Have you a better explanation?"

"Flu? That's what you told Mom," he said lamely.

"No such luck. Now what are we going to do about it?"

"We?" Donald asked, pointing to himself. "Nothing. How do I know it's not Simon Gilby's, or someone else's for that matter."

Lisa was tempted to slap him for the insult, but that was no way to accomplish her goal. Instead, she gritted her teeth, calmed herself, and then continued. "Timing, Donald. Simon has been gone over a month. There's been no one but you since. You know that, however much you want to deny it."

Donald turned away. "Lisa, you've thrown me a curve. I had no idea . . ."

"You're a big boy, Donald Hughes. You know where babies come from. It's your problem, too. It took the two of us to make this baby," she snapped.

"I know, but—"

"But what? You either take responsibility for the child or you don't. I love you and I wanted to marry you before I discovered I was pregnant. I still want to marry you. It's best for all of us now."

"All of us? I'm not so sure. The family won't understand at all."

"It's none of their business, Donald. They weren't with us when this baby was conceived. They don't have to know why we're getting married."

"They'll figure it out."

"So what? I know Nancy wouldn't want a grandchild of hers to be born out of wedlock."

"You're right. She'd be the first to tell me to do the right thing, even though she'd never approve of our marriage—under any other circumstances."

"You see," Lisa said with satisfaction. "Even *you* have to admit it would be for the best."

Donald was still tentative, but his resolve was weakening. Lisa decided another, more gentle tack was needed. She smiled and leaned against him. "I know you find me attractive, and in some small way you do love me. You could never have been so tender and caring if you didn't. We're really a matched set, Donald, you and I."

"Unfortunately, Lisa, that might very well be true. But marriage! I hadn't even thought of the possibility."

"We have to get married. For the sake of the child."

"I need to think about it," he said, drawing back.

"It'll have to be soon, Donald."

"I know," he said with resignation.

"How about next week? Carol and Tom will be back then," Lisa suggested, sensing her victory.

Donald lamely kissed her cheek. "We'll see."

After he'd left, Lisa relaxed back into the couch and clapped her hands. "My, won't everyone be surprised. I'll be Mrs. Hughes again!"

It was late that week when Bob returned home to find Jennifer waiting at the door. She was furious. Behind her, he could see Rick, gloating.

"Why didn't you tell me about what you did?" Jennifer said, before Bob even got into the house.

"What did I do?"

"You reported Rick. Said he'd tried to change your orders again. He's on probation. He might not even finish his residency."

"Did you tell her everything?" Bob asked Rick. "Or only what you thought would get you what you wanted?"

"Everything," Rick said. "You made another mistake. I found it and you had to cover for yourself. So you reported me."

"I suppose Mrs. Helstrom imagined you in C.C.U. that night?"

"I was just checking—"

"I found the beginning of a new notation on Mr. Greeley's chart, Rick. I had it locked away so you couldn't touch it again."

"See, Mom. He turns everything around. The great

and wonderful Dr. Hughes can do no wrong."

Jennifer put her hand on Rick's shoulder. "Bob, why didn't you talk to Rick about this first?"

"Twice, Jenny. Twice now! Two times too many. Can't you see he wants us to argue over him?"

"I won't have you treating my son this way. You've just about ruined his future."

"If you expect me to apologize, you've got another thing coming. He's malicious, Jenny. Why can't you see it? We can't go on like this. Every time Rick gets into trouble we have an argument. Look at him, he's enjoying every moment of this."

Bob watched Rick do a good job of looking hurt. "Mom . . ."

She was in tears. "It's not working, Bob. I need some space."

"You want a separation?"

"Under the circumstances I think it best."

When Bob had reported the incident with Rick, he knew he was risking this kind of confrontation with Jennifer, but as much as he loved her, he had his duty as a physician.

Bob moved back into the Hughes's home that evening.

The first few days of separation from Jennifer moved very slowly for Bob. To keep himself from dwelling on his problems, he spent long hours at the hospital. It was just too uncomfortable to be with his family at this time. He needed privacy to think.

Bob had no idea how to convince Jennifer that Rick needed help. She simply wouldn't listen to reason.

Although he had no appetite, Bob decided starving

himself wasn't going to accomplish anything, so he forced himself to eat some soup and a milkshake in the hospital cafeteria. He had just begun his meal when Kim entered the room.

"Bob," she said with obvious sympathy. "How are you holding up?"

"I'm managing."

"Not very well, though. Need a shoulder?"

He nodded. "Sure do. I don't know how to make things right. I can't convince Jenny that Rick is lying."

"She can't acccept that, Bob. When she lost Sean, Rick was all she had left of him. It's impossible for her to be objective right now. Just give her time."

"And what am I supposed to do in the meantime?"

"Have patience. She loves you, you know."

"I love her too, Kim, but our entire marriage has been plagued by her son from day one."

Kim nodded. "I know. It's unfortunate. But it's not hopeless, Bob. You must believe that."

There was a gentleness about Kim, a true caring which Bob appreciated. She was so calm, so easy to talk to. Everything about her made him feel better.

"I appreciate your trying to cheer me up," he said with sincerity. "You're a very special person, Kim."

"I try, kiddo. Sometimes my sister is a challenge, but take it from me, she'll come around." Kim smiled brightly.

The house seemed empty without Bob. Although Jennifer was close to the fire, she still felt cold. The light and comfort of her life had gone with Bob. She sat, staring into the flames, lost in thought.

"Jen, both of you are miserable," Kim said.

"Someone's got to make the first move. I can't stand watching you suffer so."

"Kim, it's really nothing for you to be concerned with. I didn't want to get you involved in our lives. Especially when things are so bad."

"What's a sister for? It's easy to be a fair weather friend. Want me to talk to Bob?"

"I'm sure he's miserable. Why don't you try to cheer him up at least?"

Kim smiled. Why not try to cheer him? To her distress, Kim found she wanted an excuse to be with him. "I'll give it my best shot, Jen. I only wish I could do the same for you."

"I'll work it out. Just give me some time. Rick just needs some motherly attention. He took Sean's death so hard. I'm sure he'll settle down and change his attitude. After all, he's a grown man. He can't always feel so attached to me."

Kim shrugged. "Don't encourage him, Jennifer. There's something unwholesome about his feelings for you. It's almost as if he's put himself in his father's place."

"You don't believe he really could have done what Bob accused him of."

"I love my nephew," Kim said. "But he's hurting so much, it's hard to say what he'd do. Jennifer, I'd reconsider and check more carefully before condemning Bob. He may have a point."

Jennifer was crushed. "I'd hoped you'd understand."

Kim took her sister in her arms and tried consoling her. "Oh, I do, Jen. I do understand."

Kim met Bob as he was leaving the hospital. "How

about supper at my place," she said cheerily. "You look like you could use a good meal and a pat on the back."

At first he was reluctant, but the thought of another dreary evening alone, tempered his decision. "Okay, you're on."

Bob knew Kim must have anticipated his acceptance of her invitation. As soon as they entered her new apartment, the savory aroma of a hearty stew greeted him. While he made himself comfortable in the living room, she made a pot of hot mulled cider and handed him a steamy mug before getting the meal to the table. "This'll warm your insides."

He held the mug in his hands, warming them as he looked about. Kim's apartment seemed to fit her personality. It was comfortable, attractive and not the least bit pretentious. He watched her set the table and bring a huge bowl of stew out of the kitchen. "That smells great."

"Hope you're hungry. I made enough to feed an army."

"I'm absolutely famished."

After the meal, Kim laughed as she cleared the table. "I'll say you were hungry, Bob. I've never seen anyone so ravenous."

"You do wonders for my disposition," he said cheerily. "My appetite just suddenly returned with a vengeance."

She brushed by him and he had an almost overwhelming urge to take her in his arms. He resisted the temptation and watched her move gracefully toward him. Her perfume, subtle but stimulating, suddenly filled the room. Nothing but her essence was in his mind. From the moment he'd first met Kim, he'd felt attracted to her. Now, alone with her she was an irresistible lure.

He reached for Kim and found her in his arms, willing, unresisting, returning his kisses with ardent pleasure.

"Kim," he whispered, "I love you. I think I've loved you from the first moment I set eyes on you."

Hurt showed in her eyes. "And I've loved you. I've done everything to stop myself. You're my sister's husband. She really loves you, Bob. I can't allow myself to get between you. I shouldn't have given in to my feelings tonight. It's wrong! It's dreadfully wrong!"

"You're not the cause of our problem, Kim."

"No, Bob. No matter what we feel for each other, we can't hurt her anymore. I know you love Jennifer. I'm sure you two will reconcile. You must. I couldn't live with myself if I thought I were the cause of your permanent separation." Her eyes were misty.

Bob reached for her again, but she pulled away. He could feel her resistance, her pain, as she fought her feelings.

Both of them shared the thought. *How could love, which should be so wonderful, ever be so painful?*

Dr. Stratton had been Lisa's gynecologist for years. He'd delivered Tom, and although he was getting older, she still preferred going to him. "I don't understand why I feel so awful and bloated, Doctor. I figure I'm about six weeks pregnant and I feel just terrible."

The doctor sat back, appraising his patient. He was a wise man, quiet, and very understanding. "How long have you felt this bad, Lisa?"

"Weeks. At first I thought I had the flu. But then I realized—"

131

"Have you been under any undue tension lately?"

Lisa laughed. "Lately? My life is one long period of stress!"

"I thought so," Doctor Stratton said, taking out his prescription pad. "Lisa, my examination shows you are *not* pregnant. You never have been."

"But the nausea, the other symptoms . . ."

"I believe you must really have had the flu."

"But I haven't had a period . . ."

"Stress will sometimes affect the cycle, and you must have wanted to be pregnant."

"No. I'd actually seriously considered having an abortion."

"I've known you for many years, Lisa," the doctor said calmly. "Whatever stress you're under now has caused your recent symptoms. I'm sure you'll feel better when you've solved whatever is bothering you. There's absolutely nothing physically wrong with you. I'll give you a mild tranquilizer and something which should bring on menstruation."

A bewildered Lisa left the doctor's office, wondering what she should do. *When I told Donald, I really did believe I was pregnant. What should I tell him now? He'll never marry me if he knows I'm not having his baby. He only agreed because he felt guilty and obligated. I won't tell him. After we're married, maybe. . .*

After she'd had time to digest what Dr. Stratton had told her, Lisa thought, *If I'm not pregnant with Donald's child, there might be a chance at Bob. I hear he and Jennifer have separated.* It was an appealing idea, and one that would take some consideration.

Lisa felt better already.

* * *

Bob felt even worse than he did before. He loved both Jennifer and Kim and didn't know what to do. In his heart he knew Jennifer might come to her senses and relent. He wanted that. But he wanted Kim also. He decided he needed to get away and think things out alone. There was a medical conference in Miami coming up soon. It was the perfect excuse. He could request a leave for the conference and take a short vacation on the Gulf afterwards.

But Bob soon discovered it wasn't as simple as that. Another physician had requested leave to attend the convention in Florida. Bob met John Dixon in the hospital administrator's office to work it out.

"The reason we added John Dixon to the staff was to alleviate the problem of having our only cardiologist on leave with no backup," the administrator said officiously. "Obviously, we can't allow both of you to attend the meeting in Florida."

"It's an important meeting," John said. "Dr. Helman, from Switzerland is going to report on their newest surgical technique, using a new artificial valve replacement."

The administrator turned to Bob, who said, "There's a session on new approaches to non-surgical treatment by Dr. Goldman. He's made revolutionary strides with diet."

"Possibly we could work something out. The meeting lasts a week. You could each attend only the sessions you're most interested in . . ."

"That won't work," John said, pushing the meeting's agenda onto the desk. "The sessions overlap."

"In that case, I'm afraid seniority must take precedence, Dr. Dixon. Dr. Hughes rarely requests attendance to such conferences and I must defer to his request. Possibly next time."

"You win this one, Hughes," John said through gritted teeth as they were leaving the office. "You sure made up your mind late enough."

"I didn't see it as a competition. I had no idea you had requested to go to the meeting."

"I'm sure you didn't," John said, sarcastically as he slammed the door behind him.

John Dixon planned to take full advantage of the people he'd met at the Hughes wedding. The invitation to the country club was just too good to pass up. He'd planned on going alone, but his meeting with Bob that afternoon sparked an idea.

"Kim, John Dixon here," he said after dialing her number.

"Oh, John, how nice to hear from you again." Her voice was cheery, John was encouraged.

"I'm planning to have dinner at the club tonight," he said. "I'd love you to join me."

Kim was still reeling from the reality of her love for Bob and its possible consequences. John's invitation came when she needed it most. "I'd be delighted to go."

"Eight o'clock. I'll pick you up."

John arrived exactly at eight, dressed in a dinner jacket and looking absolutely debonnaire. He seemed eager, almost jumpy as if the world just didn't turn quite fast enough for him. Kim saw that John wanted and expected a great deal out of life.

Kim knew the Hughes family had never felt the need to join the exclusive Oakdale Country Club. Nancy and Chris had never felt obligated to mix with Oakdale society at that level. They'd certainly had ample opportunity to socialize at the club, but had never once been tempted to join.

The club was elegant. Located on the lake, it offered a view of distant city lights. The club's lighting was reflected in the lake's mirrored surface, shimmering beautifully in the cold clear night.

"I hadn't realized it was so beautiful out here," Kim said as they drove up. The valet took the keys from John and they rushed into the warmth of the building. "Or that it was so cold."

"The wind makes it seem even colder than it is," John said, hugging her lightly. "How about something to warm us up?" He ordered a hot toddy for each of them.

"I didn't know you were a member here," Kim said.

"I've been nominated by a patient. I plan on paying my dues tonight. You're helping me celebrate."

"It's important to you to be part of all of this, isn't it?"

"You're damn right it is. I've had to fight my way up all of my life. I'm finally making it." Changing the subject quickly, he added, "You certainly add a touch of class to the occasion. You're absolutely breathtaking tonight."

"Why thank you, John," she said with true humility. "A lady always likes compliments."

"And you're some lady, Kim. I've never known anyone quite like you."

Kim was wearing a classic black gown with white accents, and stood out from everyone else in the room like a beacon on a dark night. John looked around the room and smiled. "You're the most elegant woman here."

He spared nothing on the dinner and when he received his membership card, he held it up for Kim to see. "This is what it's all about, Kim. I'm getting there, but I'm not all the way there yet. Wait! You'll see. Nothing is going to stop John Dixon."

When John took Kim home, she invited him up to her apartment for a nightcap. He built a fire in the fireplace to take the chill off the room, while Kim prepared some brandy over fresh fruit.

John was lying on the floor, his stockinged feet resting on the sofa. "You know, Kim, I could get used to this real easily."

She smiled in amusement. "You do look comfortable there. Sort of like a contented pup."

"Pup, eh!" He jumped up and grabbed her playfully. "I'll show you what this old dog can do." His kiss was probing, demanding, sensuous.

Kim was startled by the extent of his passion. She pulled back, causing him to hold her even tighter. "John! You're hurting me!"

He let go. "I'm sorry. It's just that I'm so overwhelmed by you. You're everything I've ever dreamed of having."

"It's just too soon to be talking this way," Kim said, backing away.

"Forgive me, Kim. I would be absolutely devastated if you don't."

"John," she said patiently. "I think I understand. You just got carried away."

"I did. I did!" He was desperate, like a little boy trying to avoid a spanking.

"Please, Kim, say you'll forgive me."

She kissed him lightly on the cheek. "There's nothing to forgive, John."

Chapter Ten
Tropical Liaison

"Bob left town without even a word to me," Jennifer told Kim. "I thought he'd at least call."

"He's hurting, Jennifer. Give him time." Kim wished she could be more encouraging to her sister, but her own guilt kept getting in the way. If Jennifer and Bob were even close to getting together again, could her involvement with Bob complicate the situation and destroy their chances? She wasn't sure she wanted to live with that over her head.

"I've decided to call it quits," Jennifer said. "Bob hasn't made a positive move, and I can't live in limbo."

"Have you called him or made any attempt to straighten out the mess?"

Jennifer nodded. "Yesterday, when Rick was reinstated."

"Does he know what he'll do when he finishes his residency at Memorial?"

"Probably join a practice in Iowa. He was offered a position with old Doctor Nance. Remember him?"

Kim smiled, remembering her childhood. "He took

my tonsils out. If it weren't for all that ice cream, I would never have forgiven him."

"He was looking for someone to share his practice and eventually take it over. It's a really good opportunity for Rick. He doesn't even have to complete the residency here to go into general practice."

Jennifer was beating around the bush, avoiding her personal plans. Kim decided to push. "And what about you?"

"To be honest, I've decided to go back with him. I've lots of old friends there. Sean was loved so . . ."

"Are you sure?"

Jennifer nodded. "I'm sure. There's nothing left for me in Oakdale."

It had just begun to snow when Kim left Jennifer's house. Her apartment wasn't far and she'd walked over. The walk back was refreshing. The snow felt wet and cold. Everything was beginning to be covered in a thin layer of cleansing white. She loved the snow. The world always seemed different when it was enveloped in a white blanket. All of the dirt was hidden.

When she got home, Kim fixed a cup of tea and turned on the television set. "The National weather picture is bleak," the forecaster reported. "Snows range from the Cascades of Washington across the Northern tier of States, through the plains and all the way to Maine. Blizzard conditions hold the Southwestern Mountains in their grip. The cold extends as far south as Georgia. Florida, however is experiencing eighty degree weather. . . ."

"Florida—Bob!" Kim said softly. "Jennifer really has no intention of reconciling. I wouldn't be interfering."

The phone rang and she reached to answer it. "Kim, John here. I'd like to make it up to you for the way our last evening ended. How about my picking you up for dinner in an hour?"

"I don't know, John."

"Please."

He sounded so distressed that Kim relented. "All right. But John, let's make it a short evening."

John kept his word. He was a perfect gentleman through the entire evening. He couldn't help but notice how distracted Kim was and asked, "Is something bothering you?"

"Oh, no, John. I'm just tired."

"I had hoped we could spend a day together, Saturday, maybe?"

Kim's answer was more direct than anything else she'd said that entire evening. "I'm sorry John. I'm planning to visit a friend for a couple of weeks. Maybe when I get back."

As soon as John dropped her off, Kim called a travel agent and arranged to be on an early morning flight from Chicago to Miami.

The meeting was as dull as Bob had anticipated. It was being held at the Fountainbleau Hotel, a pleasure palace on the Miami Beach waterfront. Coffee in the coffee shop cost a dollar and the prices went up from there.

He met some old associates and school buddies, most of whom were taking the opportunity to spend vacations with their wives. It made him feel all the more alone. To relax he took a swim in the hotel pool. It was lagoon shaped, with waterfalls coming out of artificial rock outcroppings. The pool was large enough to be a real lagoon. After his swim, he planned on turning in early with a copy of the latest medical journal. The beach was too close to ignore and Bob decided to take advantage of it while he had the opportunity. After his dip in the pool, he ventured out and dove into the warm Atlantic. After splashing around in the surf for a short time, he went back to his room and showered. He had just gotten out of the shower and wrapped a towel around his hips when he heard a knock on the door.

"Maid service."

Bob looked at the clock and frowned. "Come back tomorrow."

There was another knock.

"Okay. I'm coming." He slipped a robe on and opened the door. For a second he stared as if in shock. It was Kim!

"Well, are you going to let me in, or are you going to stand there with that silly expression on your face?"

"Kim! I didn't expect you. Come on in. When . . .?"

She laughed. "Surprised, huh?"

"That's an understatement. I'm overwhelmed. How?"

"I just flapped my arms very hard and headed south. Needed the sunshine, you know."

Once the shock of seeing her had worn off, Bob wrapped his arms tightly about Kim and kissed her. She returned his kisses without inhibition or reservation.

"The meeting lasts another three days," Bob said. "Then let's get out of here. I know a place on the Gulf."

Since many of the attending physicians knew Bob professionally, Bob and Kim decided to be discreet while at the hotel. When the meeting was over, Bob rented a car and they drove through the Everglades to the West Coast of Florida. They stopped on an Indian reservation, took a ride on an airboat through the swamps, and tried alligator burgers. One ferry ride later, they were on the tropical paradise of Sanabel Island.

The island, internationally famous, offered a relaxed, pleasant atmosphere. The white sand, covered with thousands of shells, stretched for miles. Just off the beach, a thick growth of mangroves sheltered hundreds of species of water birds. It was just the place for lovers to lose themselves.

The gulf waters were warm, and the tropical nights pleasant. Night blooming cerus, almost totally covering some of the trees, bloomed profusely, perfuming the air.

During the balmy night Kim and Bob walked the beach. There, in the moonlight, free from constraints, they found their love. The cry of the night birds and the sound of the surf were their music.

He kissed her damp hair, and she let her lips brush against his bare chest, finally meeting his mouth in a fervent kiss. The gentle surf washed onto the beach, churning an even rhythm.

"Forever," Bob whispered. "This night will be forever."

Kim looked up and sighed. "As long as the moon shines, my love."

They embraced again and the tropical night covered them with its warmth. Oakdale and its problems vanished as the lovers created their own perfect world.

The silver Porsche drove past Carol and Tom, then stopped. Disregarding traffic, the driver backed up.

"Tom!"

Tom turned and looked to see who was calling. "Meredith!"

Meredith pulled over to the curb and looked Carol up and down. "Tom, Simon and I are in town for a short time. How about dinner tonight?"

She seemed to have forgotten about Greg, Carol noticed, but she had the sense not to say anything. Let Meredith put her foot in her mouth. She didn't seem to need any help.

"Meredith," Tom said, savoring the moment. "Do you remember Carol?"

Meredith remembered something about the mouse Tom had been dating before she'd met him. She still wasn't any competition. "No."

Tom smiled broadly and said, "This is my wife, Carol."

Meredith looked stunned.

Carol enjoyed Meredith's surprise as much as Tom did. "What a suprise to see you again."

"Quite a surprise," Meredith responded weakly.

"Well," Tom said. "Bye Meredith. It was nice seeing you again."

Meredith shrugged her shoulders, and waved as she drove off.

This time, Tom knew, the wave, was a final farewell.

Tom hugged Carol and they walked on happily together.

When he returned from his trip, Bob's service had a number of messages for him. He'd left Kim in Florida. She'd decided it was best they not return to Oakdale together. There was time enough to tell everyone about their love, after his divorce from Jennifer. Bob shuffled through the messages, deciding that only one person needed an immediate response. It seemed Jennifer had been calling his service daily for the past four days.

He crunched through the snow up to the walk, wondering how his home could seem so strange to him. It was as if he'd been gone for an eternity. So many things had changed since he'd left just a month before. Now he felt out of place here.

Jennifer answered the door. She looked at peace, serene. He wondered what could have changed her so. The last time he'd seen her there had been no reasoning with her.

"Jenny, I got your messages. I was in Florida, at a meeting."

"I know," she said. "Mom Hughes told me you were taking a vacation afterwards." He looked tanned and relaxed. "I see it did you some good."

"I needed the break."

"Bob . . ." She seemed to be having a hard time saying what she'd intended. "I've asked Rick to leave town. He's back in Iowa."

"He didn't finish his residency?"

"It wasn't necessary to go into general practice."

"And he left willingly?"

"It took some persuasion. Bob, I love you. I never wanted to hurt you."

"I know, Jenny. Sometimes our kids have a way of demanding things from us in a way we can't ignore."

"Yes, they do," she said smiling knowingly. "Sit down, Bob. There's something I have to tell you."

Bob knew what she was going to say, and his heart pounded. How could he tell her he was in love with her sister, Kim? But he still loved Jennifer too. Seeing her again reminded him of that. She was still that wonderful, warm, loving woman he'd married. How could he not want his marriage to be repaired? How could he choose between them?

Jennifer looked into his eyes and smiled. "Bob, I'm pregnant. I'm going to have our baby."

"Baby," he repeated. "A baby? Jenny, that's wonderful!"

"I'd hoped you'd feel that way. Bob, I want this child. It means a great deal to me. It cements our love for each other. I don't know what I was thinking when Rick came to me. I was wrong to believe him. He was so confused. He needed me so much. I completely lost perspective. It's you and me. We're what counts. No one, except us and our child."

"Our child," he whispered. "When?"

"Late October. Halloween!"

The choice had been made for him. He couldn't turn away from his wife, not when she was expecting their child. He took Jennifer into his arms and they celebrated their love for each other and the future's happy prospects.

Nobody was happier than Nancy Hughes. Another grandchild! And Bob and Jennifer were together again. The entire family was invited to a reunion dinner.

Nancy never approved of divorce. It was a necessary evil one lived with but it was to be avoided if possible. Bob and Jennifer never seemed happier. A child, the fruit of their love, was all it took to make things right.

"How wonderful," Nancy said, bringing a large chocolate cake out of the kitchen. For obvious reasons, it was heart shaped. "Tom, Carol, you're next to make a happy announcement," Nancy said, beaming with anticipation at the thought of a great grandchild.

Carol blushed, and they all laughed.

When the meal was finished and everyone was near to bursting, Chris stood at the head of the table, facing his family and offered a toast. "To all of the generations of the Hughes family. May they always be this happy."

All was going well on the home front, but it wasn't at all that smooth for Bob at the hospital. When he arrived back at Memorial he found there had been some problems with one of his patients. His nurse knew that he wouldn't at all approve of what was done. She handed him the chart and quickly rushed off, knowing an explosion was to follow.

"What's this?" Bob demanded. "Helen, what the hell is going on?"

"He was admitted the day after you left for Florida."

"I can see that," Bob said, waving the chart at her. "Why wasn't I called?"

"Dr. Dixon was on call and admitted him. He didn't think it was necessary, Doctor."

"Didn't think it was necessary? With my patient? Get me Dr. Dixon," Bob stormed. "Have him in my office. Immediately."

Helen made a quick exit and called John's office.

In one hour John was standing in front of Bob's desk. He looked very pleased with himself and not at all disturbed. "Something you wanted to say to me?" he asked lightly.

"You operated on one of my patients without checking with me?" Bob asked in an accusatory tone.

"It was an emergency," John said. "You were a thousand miles away. It was your choice to go to the conference," he jabbed. "You'd have done the same in my place."

"Surgery wasn't indicated."

"I disagree. It definitely should have been performed earlier."

"That's a matter of opinion."

"Look here," John said. "So we don't think alike. That's not too bad. After all, maybe our patients will benefit from our differences."

"Not when you're so quick with the knife. Trying to beef up your fees, Doctor Dixon? Is that how you can afford the country club?"

"That's a low blow," John shouted. "Your overly cautious measures jeopardize your patients' lives."

"Surgery is an unnecessary risk in most cases. Medical techniques have proven just as effective. With diet and exercise we can avoid most surgeries."

"I disagree. Surgery alleviates the problem immediately."

"But at much greater risk."

It was an argument which they'd had before and would have again. Different philosophies of treatment were not uncommon among associates, but in their case personalities also played an important factor. Neither Bob nor John would give an inch.

Their shouting carried into the outer office and into the hall. By the time a fuming John left Bob's office, the entire staff was aware of their heated argument.

Bob acted quickly and went to the hospital Board to ask for John's removal from the staff. The Board called an immediate session to consider his request. Both Bob and John were called to argue their cases.

John stood next to Bob, looking like he'd been the injured party. Bob couldn't help but think the man was a great actor.

"We simply can't tolerate such a contentious man on staff," Bob argued. "He had no right to operate on my patient without my consent."

"I was on call. I considered it an emergency situation," John explained. "I didn't have time to fool around with phone calls . . ."

"A phone call is not too much to ask," Bob said. "It's not as if you have to tap the message out in code or send up smoke signals, John."

"It was my decision to make, and I made it," John said clearly and distinctly. "I'll make no apologies for a job well done. You're in the wrong. Your conservatism could have been the death of that man."

"He could have died in surgery."

The hospital administrator turned to John. "How is the patient in question doing?"

"He's recovering well. I'd say he'll be able to leave Memorial in just a few days."

"Medical procedures would have accomplished the same without such great risk," Bob interjected.

The opposing doctors were asked to leave while the Board deliberated. After a few tense minutes they were asked to return to hear the decision.

"Doctor Hughes, Doctor Dixon is a highly qualified surgeon and a well-known specialist in the field of cardiology. He is here because of his excellent credentials and is, as far as we can determine, an asset to Memorial. In this case, he used his judgment in an emergency to the patient's benefit as far as we can tell. We see no reason to take action. We do, however, recommend the two of you work out your differences before your disagreements actually do affect the welfare of your patients."

As they were leaving Bob turned to John. "You've won this time. But sometime you're going to get knife happy and botch up."

"It'll be a cold day in hell when I do," John said. "Just watch out, Hughes. I don't take to this kind of treatment lightly. I'll get my turn. Just wait and see."

As soon as Kim returned from Florida, Jennifer invited her to dinner. With such good news to tell, she didn't want a minute's delay. Kim had mixed feelings about accepting the invitation, but she and Bob had agreed before he left Florida to be discreet until his situation with Jennifer was resolved. Rather than bring attention to her discomfort about the situation, Kim accepted Jennifer's invitation.

When Bob arrived home that evening, Kim was sitting in the living room with Jennifer. He didn't quite know how to face her. The battle with John had been trying, and he couldn't bear an evening of tension as well, but there was no choice. He smiled and joined them.

"Hi, Kim," he said as nonchalantly as he could. "Have a good trip?"

"Yes," she answered quietly. "I had a marvelous time. I love the Caribbean."

"The both of you are so tanned you make all of us in Oakdale look like a bunch of ghosts" Jennifer said cheerily. "Next time you go on one of the medical junkets, Bob, I'm going to insist upon coming with you."

He forced a smile, all the while looking at Kim to see her reaction. Kim's gaze went from Bob to Jennifer and she realized what was going on. Somehow, they'd made peace with each other again.

"Kim just arrived," Jennifer explained. "I haven't told her all our good news yet."

"I can see for myself," Kim said. "I'm so glad you've been able to settle your differences. I told you it would work out, Jen, didn't I?"

"But our reconciliation is only part of it, Kim. Tell her, Bob?"

Bob, feeling weak in the knees, sat down on the couch. He just couldn't tell Kim. "I wanted you to be the one to tell her, Jenny."

Jennifer was just bursting with happiness. "Kim we're expecting a child. It's due in the fall. Isn't that wonderful?"

Kim smiled sincerely. "That's terrific. I'm going to have a little niece or nephew to spoil. Bob, I know how happy you must be."

"He's ecstatic about it and so am I," Jennifer said, saving Bob from answering. He couldn't have if he'd tried, with his heart in his mouth as it was.

"Congratulations," Kim said, smiling sweetly. "I can see how happy and how much in love you two are. It couldn't have happened to two more wonderful people. I love you both."

Although it was completely unintentional on Kim's part, Bob felt as if she'd stabbed him with a sharp knife.

The trip to the doctor had been pending ever since Kim

had arrived back in Oakdale. She'd not been feeling up to par and felt a checkup was called for. She'd chosen Dr. Brawley, an internist at Memorial who came highly recommended.

"Miss Reynolds, your tests have come back from the lab," Dr. Brawley said, as he leaned forward. He seemed nervous, disturbed about something.

"Yes?" Kim said, wondering what could be wrong with her.

"One of your tests proved positive."

"Positive? What are you trying to tell me, Doctor?"

"That you're pregnant, Miss Reynolds. The tests also show you're just slightly anemic, but that's not serious. It may be the reason you've felt listless, but my guess is the pregnancy is the more likely factor."

"But I can't be . . ."

The doctor cocked his head. "It's very early. You probably haven't been aware of the time."

"I haven't checked." She put her hands to her head. "My Lord, I hadn't even considered the possibility. Are you sure? If it's so early maybe it's false . . ."

He shook his head. "The test is valid, Miss Reynolds. It's definite. From your reaction, I would say it wasn't planned?"

She nodded. "No. But don't misunderstand my reaction. I want the child. I'd never think of not having it."

"Good," Dr. Brawley said, seemingly pleased with her decision. "In that case, I'll recommend a gynecologist. Dr. Olson is a good man on staff here."

Kim remembered Jennifer mentioning Dr. Olson. "I prefer to see a physician not on the Memorial staff," she said firmly.

"I understand," Dr. Brawley replied with a nod. He recommended a doctor on the staff of Faith Hospital and had an appointment set up for Kim.

Although it was frigid and was snowing heavily, Kim drove to the lake. She needed to be completely alone to think. The path along the lake was covered with about three inches of snow when she began to walk. She'd wrapped her fur coat tightly about her and was wearing a hat to match, so the cold didn't bother her much.

The blizzard somehow comforted her, its turmoil matching hers.

Should she tell Bob? she wondered. Now that he was back with Jennifer could she risk ruining their happiness? Could she risk ruining *Bob's* happiness?

"I love him so much," she shouted to the gale. "I can't hurt him. I can't hurt Jennifer either. I love them both too much. I just can't tell him. He must never know. I want this child. It's all I'll ever have of his love."

She trudged back to the car and turned to see her lone tracks in the deepening snow.

"Kim!" John ran into Kim in the hospital cafeteria and sat down next to her. "I haven't seen you since you got back from your trip." He noticed the medical file folder on the table. "You all right? You're not ill, are you?"

"I'm fine, John. Just picking up some old medical records to transfer."

"Oh?" he said, curious for more information. When none was forthcoming, he changed the subject. "I'm going to take you up on that date you turned down before you left. How are you fixed for tonight?"

"I thought I'd curl up with a good book in front of the fire and just keep warm."

"Your fire or mine?" John said eagerly. "I'll even cook."

Kim really didn't feel up to company. "I don't know, John."

"You gonna make me beg?" He knelt down for a silly joke.

Kim covered her eyes, frustrated and somewhat flustered. "Okay, John. Now, please, get up before you make a spectacle of both of us."

"That was exactly my intention," he said, laughing. "I want everyone to see us together." Thinking of Bob's reaction, he smiled. It had to be galling Bob to have his sister-in-law dating John Dixon. Besides, he really liked Kim, so it made it all the better.

Preferring not to go out into the bad weather again, Kim suggested John come to her place. Ready and willing, he arrived laden with boxes of Chinese food. But after he'd served the first course, John noticed that her appetite wasn't quite up to par.

"Are you sure you're all right? You're hardly eating a thing. Why did you visit the hospital today? You're not ill?"

"I told you I was there to pick up my records, John. Let's just drop the subject, please. I ate so much on my trip, I decided to cut down when I got home. That's all."

John surveyed her and commented, "You don't look as if you've put on an inch. In fact, you're perfect the way you are. I'm usually prescribing diets for my patients. Take it from me, if you were one of them I wouldn't recommend losing one single pound."

"Thanks, but I really prefer not to eat too much."

"Have it your way," he said, digging into the spareribs. "It's really good, though. You don't know what you're missing."

Kim realized John's heart was in the right place. He really did seem sincerely concerned about her. Right now she needed someone who cared. She felt so alone.

After dinner, Kim joined John for tea and an almond cookie. He poured brandy and offered her one.

"Not tonight," she answered. "The tea is fine."

John wondered why she refused the drink, but decided not to force the issue. She was too sensitive about his questions. He decided it was best to let Kim relax with him rather than press her about anything this evening. As the evening progressed, Kim seemed less upset.

"You know, Kim, I really enjoy being with you. You're good for me. You complement me. I'm sort of abrasive."

She looked at him and raised her brow and smiled. "I'll say."

"I know I'm hard to get along with. I'm a fighter and I scare everyone to death with my aggressiveness. But I mean well. I really do, Kim."

"I realize that, John. You do tend to put people off, though. I know it's important to you to get ahead socially, but if you really want to do that you'll have to work on some of those hard edges of yours."

"Will you help me?"

"I—I don't know, John."

"I can't think of anyone better. You're just the one. Everyone likes you," he said, snuggling closer "I think I'm beginning to more than *like* you."

She looked off into the fire, her eyes focused far beyond the flames.

John knew something was really bothering her. "Kim, if you need someone to talk to . . ."

She smiled and kissed him tenderly on the cheek. "Thanks, John. Right now all I need is a friend."

"If ever you need me, just holler," he said, returning her gentle kiss. John smiled and took her in his arms. He wanted to comfort her, to really understand what was troubling her. Patience, not one of his virtues, was what was needed. He forced himself to keep his questions to himself.

Kim moved closer and put her head in his lap. "You really are a good friend, John."

Chapter Eleven
Love's Choices

Lisa was out shopping. Since it was one of her favorite pastimes, she intended to make a day of it. There was so much to do before her wedding. Even though she'd agreed with Donald to keep it simple, she couldn't resist splurging. The occasion most definitely required a special dress, and of course there were the flowers and all of the other arrangements to be made. She'd just about decided to let Bob give the bride away. That would add a nice touch. Not many ex-husbands had that kind of an opportunity, she thought, laughing.

Lisa skimmed through the dresses on the rack of the most exclusive boutique in town. Cost was no object. Her two previous marriages had made her quite comfortable. *What color? Certainly not white*, she thought. She looked at a blue dress. A mid-winter wedding . . . maybe blue. But decided it was too mundane and headed for another rack. Then she saw it, the perfect thing: a subtle pink, silk brocade suit with beading on the collar and down the lapel. Elegant, simple, but absolutely marvelous. She tried it on. It fit as if it were made for her and she bought it on the spot. Finding a hat to go with it was fun. She finally chose a small matching creation with a little veil and a pearl clip. Then she bought matching shoes.

This was a glorious day. She treated herself to a luxurious lunch in the Colonnade Room, then planned on stopping at Nancy's and showing off her newly purchased treasures.

Nancy was busy in the kitchen when Lisa arrived. If Nancy wasn't in her kitchen, the world would be completely out of kilter, Lisa thought with amusement.

A cup of coffee appeared as if by magic and Nancy produced a still warm coffee cake. "I've just about got the house all straightened out for the wedding. I've ordered red carnations. I know you love red."

"Oh, I do," Lisa said. "I'll have red roses for my bouquet. Everything's going to be perfect."

"I've fixed some hors d'oeuvres and put them in the freezer, and I should have the cake baked tomorrow. I'll decorate it the morning of the wedding. I've planned on a white cake with orange flavored frosting. Is that all right with you, Lisa?"

"I didn't want you to have to fuss with the food," Lisa said, knowing Nancy would have a fit when she told her of her plans, "so I arranged to have the whole thing catered."

"Lisa, that was unnecessary. It's a small wedding. No bother at all."

"The mother of the groom shouldn't have to work on her son's wedding day. No, I insist. Besides, I've already placed the order."

When Lisa made up her mind there was no use

arguing. Knowing it was hopeless to try, Nancy relented. "All right, if you insist, but I still think it's a terrible waste of money," she added.

"Everything is going so well," Lisa told her, while her mind contemplated other things.

Lisa had invited Donald over for dinner. The wedding was only days away and they had so much to talk about. They hadn't even discussed a honeymoon yet. Naturally, Lisa had quite a few ideas on that.

"Nancy, what do you think of Hawaii for a honeymoon?" she asked. "I've never been there."

She couldn't wait for the evening to come so that she could firm up her plans with Donald.

Bob literally ran into Dr. Stratton in the lobby. They bumped as Dr. Stratton rushed by on his way to the delivery room. The charts Stratton was carrying scattered through the lobby as the draft coming from the constantly opening door caught them.

Stratton hurriedly scooped up the papers, pecking at them like some agitated hen as he scrambled about the lobby. "I've got a patient about to deliver—"

"It's my fault," Bob said. "I'll collect them and get them to your office later today."

"Thanks, Bob, I really appreciate that," Stratton said as he dashed off.

With the help of one of the hospital volunteers, Bob collected all the charts and he was on his way into the elevator in minutes. The papers were all in disarray and would need to be sorted. Bob planned on putting Helen to that chore.

As he stood in the elevator he began to browse through the charts. On one of the folders, he saw the name Lisa Shea. Ethics required he put the folder away and not open it, but he simply couldn't resist just one quick peek.

"Diagnosis: false pregnancy brought on by stress."

Bob took the chart into his office and read through it. Is this why Donald changed his mind and said he'd marry Lisa, he wondered? Did she tell him she was pregnant? He wondered. But then, when she found out she wasn't . . . He knew Lisa too well. "Damn that bitch," he said aloud. *I'll bet she kept that little tidbit to herself and Donald still thinks she's pregnant. It's not too late. The wedding's two days off.*

He reached for the intercom. "Helen, call my brother, Donald, and tell him it's important I see him right away."

It really seemed it was Bob's day to be involved in other people's business. When he saw Kim having lunch with John in the cafeteria he couldn't help but feel angry. "What does she see in him?" he muttered.

That evening, Bob stopped by Kim's apartment. When she opened the door to him, she was totally surprised. "Bob, what are you doing here?"

"I had to talk to you, Kim. I saw you with John Dixon at lunch today, and you were out to dinner with him last night. You're seeing a great deal of him these days."

"Yes, but that's not really your concern."

"But he's so slimy, Kim. I hate the way he oils his way around you."

"He's been a good friend when I needed one, Bob. I don't intend to be alone forever."

"But John! Good God, Kim, there are lots of other men out there. Why him?"

Bob noticed she looked very tired. It was much too early for sleep, but she was obviously dressed for bed.

"I need someone, Bob. Someone who is right here and cares about me. I can't be alone just now."

He worried about the way she looked. "Why? What are you keeping from me? Are you ill?"

"No. I'm fine, really."

"You're not a very good liar, Kim. You get a strange far-away look on your face when you're not being quite honest. Your eyes become unfocused. I see that look in your face now. Tell me. What's wrong?"

Kim sank down onto the couch. "You'll know sooner or later," she said with resignation.

"Then you are ill. I knew it. Is it serious?"

"Bob, it's nothing like that. I'm pregnant."

"Oh, my God! It's mine, isn't it?"

She nodded. "I really want this baby. It's all I'll ever have of you, Bob."

"You and Jennifer too!" He looked dazed and disoriented.

"Bob, it's all right." Kim put a hand on his shoulder to comfort him.

"Oh, Kim, I'm so sorry."

"About creating a new life? About our love? There's nothing wrong with either of them. There's absolutely nothing to be sorry about."

"I can't be a real father to the baby. It's wrong to leave you alone like this when I love you. Besides, you need me."

Kim's voice was soft and calm. "Jennifer needs you too. She also loves you, and she's your wife. I can't hurt her, and I know you don't want her hurt either. I'll get along fine."

"Kim, you're not thinking of marrying John? Does he know about the baby?"

"No, but it won't be long until it becomes obvious to everyone. I won't tell anyone who the father is. That's between us."

"But Jennifer."

"For God's sake, don't tell her. It would only destroy what you two have found again."

He knew Kim was right. They couldn't tell Jennifer, not when things were going so well for them and she was so happy.

"I have to do something. I'll help you financially. Set up a trust."

"For your niece or nephew," she reminded him. "Not your child, Bob. Thank you, but it's best you don't do anything."

"I love you, Kim. I always will. I just can't ignore this."

"You must. For all our sakes."

"How could this have happened," he cried. "I love you both so much I couldn't choose between you. Now you're both pregnant by me."

There was nothing Kim could say to comfort him, she simply watched him leave, a troubled, unhappy man.

Lisa had prepared a small feast for Donald. The small table was sparkling with crystal and her best china was laid out on a brand new linen tablecloth. Candles in crystal holders waited to be lit. Everything was ready. She slipped on a red silk dress, adjusted a stray hair and approved of the result.

When Lisa opened the door for him, Donald pushed into the room like an angry storm.

"Donald! What's wrong?"

"What's wrong, Lisa? What could be wrong? Everything's just the way you want it. Is that right?"

"Why, yes."

"And you can't imagine why I'd be angry with you, now could you?"

"Of course not. Donald, why are you behaving this way? I've never seen you this upset. Is it premarital jitters or something?"

"It's definitely something , Lisa. You've been lying to me all along, haven't you?"

"Lying?" Her face paled. "Why, Donald, I have no idea of what you're talking about."

"Oh, don't you." He grabbed her arm and pushed her down onto the couch. "You don't have the slightest idea, do you?"

"No."

"You just thought that we'd get married first, then you'd tell me you weren't pregnant. Do I have that straight, Lisa my dear?"

"How did you . . ?"

"So, I'm right! You aren't pregnant are you? You set a nice neat little trap, didn't you. And I stuck my big foot right into it."

"Who told you? Nobody knew. I . . . I . . ."

"Never mind. It doesn't matter how I found out. An accident. A very lucky accident."

"But you do love me, Donald. What difference does it make if you truly love me."

"You really don't see any difference do you? As long as you get your way, everything's fair. Everyone warned me about you, and your schemes, but I had to learn for myself. It's all true. Everything everyone's ever said ever said about you, and more."

"But Donald, let me explain."

He laughed bitterly, "You really think you can?"

"It all started so innocently. I *did* think I was pregnant, Donald. I really did. I was late, very late. I felt so awful . . . When I finally went to the doctor he told me I wasn't pregnant after all. I just couldn't disappoint you—"

"Disappoint me? What were you thinking, Lisa. How long did you think you'd keep me from knowing? Didn't you think it would become obvious after a while?"

"After a while, but by then we'd be married and have each other. It wouldn't seem so bad then."

"I can't believe this!" he shouted. "I think you've really convinced yourself you've done this for my sake. But I don't buy it, Lisa. Whatever anyone says, I'll never believe you didn't plan the whole deception from the very beginning."

"But Donald, I didn't. I really didn't. It just sort of got out of hand . . . You'll forgive me, won't you?"

"No, Lisa. I won't, and I definitely won't marry you either."

"But the wedding, all of the plans. What will you tell everyone?"

"I'm not going to tell anyone anything. You're the one who's going to have to cancel everything. Let's just see how you explain it all to them?"

"But Donald, I couldn't. I just couldn't."

"I could kill you for this," Donald said coldly.

Donald left and slammed the door so hard it bounced back open, permitting the swirling snow to blast into the house.

* * *

The weather had cleared. Rain wet fields shone brightly in the light of a full moon. In the car driving back from Chicago with John, Kim was very quiet. She looked out the window at the vast plains, feeling desolate.

"A penny for your thoughts," John said in an attempt to draw her out.

"I don't think my thoughts would be worth that much."

"Don't put yourself down, Kim. You're one of the sharpest ladies I've ever met."

"Thanks John, but right now that's not very much consolation."

"You've been off somewhere on Mars for weeks," he said. "I wonder if you even saw the play tonight."

"I didn't think it was that obvious."

"Lady, take it from me. Since you came back from that trip you took in February, you've been out of it. I know you need someone to talk to? How about my shoulder to lean on?"

She hadn't had anyone to share her problems with and had been feeling all alone in the world. In the sheltering dark, driving along the country roads, unable to clearly see the person she was confiding in, Kim felt less vulnerable.

"John. . . ?"

"Yes," he said softly, offering her much-needed encouragement.

"I do have something to tell you. I hope you'll understand . . ."

"Haven't I always?"

He has, she thought. *Bob is wrong about John. I can trust him.* Just being able to tell someone who wasn't intimately involved was a relief. "John, I'm pregnant."

For a moment John didn't know what to say. Finally he asked, "Do I know the father?"

"I don't want to talk about him," Kim said defensively.

"Not one of the more noble types, I gather? What do you plan on doing?"

"I'm going to have the baby, of course. I have no other choice. It's almost twelve weeks now."

"You wouldn't consider an abortion? It's still possible."

"Absolutely not. It never was an option. I want this child."

"Oh," John said. "You still have an attachment to the father."

"No!" she said too sharply.

John smiled. She definitely was sensitive on that subject. He decided not to push it.

Kim didn't want John probing any further. "John, I appreciate the shoulder, but do you mind if we don't talk about this anymore?"

"Sure, anything you want."

After he dropped Kim off, John had a lot of thinking to do. He put his fine diagnostician's mind to work on the problem, examining what he knew of the facts.

Twelve weeks, he thought back. *She must have met the man on her trip.* He knew it wasn't like Kim to just take to any stranger. The man had to be special. Then he re-evaluated.

Maybe the man hadn't been a stranger after all. If not a stranger, then whom? Twelve weeks. The medical conference in Florida was about that same time. Late March, early April. Hmmm. Bob Hughes was at the conference. Come to think of it they were both gone at the same time. A coincidence? John wondered.

But the more John thought about the possiblity, the more it seemed plausible. *They were gone at the same time. Kim left a few days after Bob and returned a week after he did. Bob and Jennifer were separated at the time. Kim wouldn't have felt she were interfering in their relationship.*

It pleased John to think of Bob as the villain, even if it weren't true. *So, the wonderful Dr. Bob may not be such a saint after all,* he thought. *Well, what do you know about that? There's just got to be a way I can use this. First I have to confirm my suspicions. Oh, how I'd like to get something like this on the self righteous Dr. Hughes. But how do I get it out of Kim . . .?*

In early spring, weather permitting, Nancy preferred to serve Sunday brunch in the garden. The Hughes garden was Grandpa Hughes's territory and was a work of art. Not a blade of grass was out of place. Tulips, daffodils and hyacinths bloomed along the edge of the grass, and the large willow, just leafing out, and still a light green, shaded the patio.

Tom and Carol had arrived early. Tom helped Grandpa arrange the chairs around the large patio table, while Carol helped Nancy in the kitchen.

"Carol, dear," Nancy said. "Would you get the eggs out of the refrigerator, please."

"I've never made omelets," Carol said.

"It's easy. I don't even need a recipe. Just watch." Nancy liked her new granddaughter. Her sweetness hadn't changed with her marriage to Tom; if anything, she seemed to be even more delightful.

"Mom! You in the kitchen?" It was Bob, juggling a bag of oranges and some pots Jennifer had borrowed from Nancy.

Nancy laughed. "Now where else would I be?"

"I baked coffee cake," Jennifer said, putting a nut and fruit laden confection on the table.

"You didn't have to do that," Nancy said.

"No, but I wanted to." She kissed Nancy on the cheek. "That's for being such a good mother and having such a great son."

Bob laughed and pointed at his cheek. "Hey, what about me?"

"Feeling neglected, huh?" Jennifer crossed the room and planted a juicy kiss on his lips. "There's always one left over for you, dear."

This is the way it's supposed to be, Nancy thought, as she watched Bob and Jennifer's exchange. The doorbell rang. "Will you get that please, Carol," she asked. Carol's hands were full, so Bob said, "I'll get it," and dashed to the front door. He opened it and stared for a moment before saying anything. "Kim! I didn't know you were going to be here today."

Kim could see they were alone for the moment. "We can't always avoid each other. They'll notice something is peculiar."

"How are you," Bob asked, glancing behind to make sure they were still alone. "I haven't seen you for so long. . . ."

"Coming along. I'm feeling fine, Bob. Don't worry about me."

"Kim!" Jennifer called. "Where have you been keeping yourself? You haven't been to the house in ages."

"I've been busy," Kim said. "It's amazing how time goes by so quickly."

After a few minutes of conversation they all walked to the patio where Nancy began serving. "Kim, I'm so glad you could come. You've been such a stranger. I'd hoped we'd have an opportunity to see more of you."

"I really appreciated the invitation," Kim said.

"You don't need an invitation, dear. You're part of the family." Nancy looked carefully at Kim and then commented. "You're looking wonderful. Why you're absolutely glowing, and you've put on a few pounds. Good. This emaciated look that's so popular now is simply not healthy."

"Mom," Bob said. "You'd like it if everybody were ten pounds overweight."

"Well, I always say there's nothing wrong with a good healthy look. Now, sit down and eat before everything gets cold."

After brunch, Jennifer had a few moments alone with Kim. "I wasn't joking," she said. "If I didn't know you better, I'd think you were purposely avoiding Bob and me."

"Don't be silly," Kim said. "You know how much I love you both." She indicated Jennifer's bulging tummy and smiled. "I certainly have no intention of missing any opportunity to see that nephew or niece of mine developing. How are you feeling, Jen?"

"Great. I never thought a pregnancy could be this easy. It's much better than my first."

"How is Rick?"

"Doing well. Doctor Nance is really pleased with his work. Maybe it was the best solution for him after all."

"You see, I told you it would work out for the best,"

Kim said.

"You're such an optimist. How did I ever deserve such a wonderful sister?" Jen put an arm around Kim.

"That's mutual, kiddo."

"By the way, Kim. Nancy's right." Jennifer said. "You do seem to have put on a few pounds."

"Yes, well," Kim hedged. "You know how it is."

"I hate to spoil the day for you," Jennifer said seriously when she and Kim were alone. "But Bob said you were seeing a great deal of John Dixon lately. Is that true?"

"Why yes. John's a good friend."

"Kim, I work with him, and he's anything but. He's an opportunist. Watch out for him."

"Why is everybody so down on John? He's been wonderful to me."

"He can be as smooth as silk one minute and a viper the next."

"That's just not so, Jen. He's a little rough around the edges, maybe, but he's trying to improve. He's really been good to me."

"That's because he's ambitious. I believe he won't let anything stand in his way."

"That's the great American way, Sis. What's wrong with wanting to get ahead?"

"Nothing. If one doesn't step on others on the way up."

"I think you're overreacting because Bob and John disagree so frequently."

"Bob's worried about you too."

"Jennifer, I appreciate how much you both care for me, but I'm quite capable of living my own life. I like John. I intend to continue seeing him. I'd appreciate it if you would leave us alone."

"All right, Kim. But if you ever need me."

Kim smiled. "Thanks, Jen. I'll remember that."

"Kim," John said, handing her a plate of food. "I've been thinking seriously about our talk the other night."

"I wish you'd forget what I told you completely."

"You're going to be showing soon. In fact, I think you are now, just a bit."

"Nancy Hughes noticed I'd put on weight. It's just a matter of time."

"The father of the child didn't offer to marry you?"

"He can't."

"Married?"

She bit her lip.

"I thought so. You know, Kim, I've been thinking, and I've put two and two together. It's Bob Hughes, isn't it? That trip to the Caribbean ended up in Florida, didn't it?"

"I'd rather not discuss it."

"I'm right, aren't I? It is Bob. Your sister's husband. I gather Jennifer doesn't know. Does Bob?"

She nodded.

"He does. Well, I guess you two have discussed what you should do?"

"I don't want Jennifer hurt."

"But you want the child. Have you ever thought about all of the questions that will pop up once it becomes obvious you're pregnant?" John could see the tears welling in Kim's eyes. "Don't cry, Kim. Doctor John has the prescription."

"I haven't been able to come up with anything," Kim said, sniffling.

John offered her his handkerchief. "Marry me. Everyone will think the child is mine."

"But I couldn't ask that of you."

"You're not. It's my idea. We make a good team, don't we. I love you, Kim. All these months we've been seeing each other have made me see that. I really want you, baby or no baby, it doesn't matter."

"I—I—don't know. I hadn't thought . . ."

"Don't think. Do. We can go off to Maryland and be back in a flesh as Dr. and Mrs. John Dixon. That isn't such a bad idea, is it?"

"Oh, John, of course it isn't. I do like you, but marriage is such a big step."

"Tonight, Kim. Let's fly out tonight."

"But, John, it's so soon . . ."

"What should we wait for? I love you, you like me. We'll make it work. Well, what do you say?"

"I'm overwhelmed."

"Then let's do it!"

"All right. Let's."

That night Kim and John caught the late flight to Baltimore. They were married in a civil ceremony at a wedding chapel near the airport and returned to Oakdale immediately after.

Kim called Jennifer as soon as she and John returned to Oakdale. "Can I come over for a few minutes. We have to talk."

"You know you don't have to ask," Jennifer said. "I'm not heading into the hospital until later. How about a late breakfast?"

"Thanks, but I won't have much time. I just want to talk."

Jennifer knew Kim well enough to know she had something important to say. Kim had a way of getting very quiet when there was something brewing. Her voice over the phone was a definite clue, but what could it be?

"Well, what's up?" Jennifer asked as Kim came into the house.

Kim held her left hand out to her sister, displaying a gold wedding band.

"John?" Jennifer asked, knowing the answer. "When?"

"Last night. In Maryland. We just got back."

"Does anyone else know?"

"Not yet, there hasn't been time. Jennifer, aren't you going to at least congratulate me?"

"Of course, Honey. I don't know what I was thinking. I hope you'll be very happy." The expression on her face didn't match her words. "I'm not so sure how Bob will take this though. He and John aren't the best combination in the world."

"I hope they can mend their differences," Kim said. "They really have a great deal in common."

Kim was thinking how much in common they really had and was concerned about how Bob would react to John's becoming the legal father of his child. She was sure he wasn't going to be very pleased about it but hoped he'd understand her motivation for the marriage. It was done. There was nothing he could do about it anyway.

Chapter Twelve
Silences

When the phone rang Kim seriously considered not answering it. She sat on her bed listening to it and wondering whether she should give in to her urge to smash it and have done with it completely. It had to be John, and she wasn't in the mood to contend with another of his demands. But if she didn't answer it, she knew she was in for another tirade, so she finally picked it up. Her voice clearly indicated her anger.

"Hello, Kim here."

"Kim, it's Jennifer." When the line remained silent, she became alarmed. "Kim! Are you all right?"

Kim certainly didn't want Jennifer or Bob to know of her problems with John. "I'm fine. You caught me as I was leaving the house."

"You sound disturbed. Are you sure?"

"Jennifer, when are you ever going to stop worrying about me?"

"Probably never."

"It's my turn then. How are you doing?"

"Dr. Stratton says everything's coming along well. I'm

due in November," she said, distractedly.

"Looks like we'll be pretty close."

"How's John holding up?"

"John? He's okay. Why did you ask?"

From Kim's reaction, Jennifer realized John must have been the cause of her sister's strange behavior. "Kim, is everything all right between you and John?"

"Whatever gave you the idea there might be a problem?"

"Intuition. Bob and I haven't seen much of you two since you've been married."

"We've been very busy. John's really active at the club and feels it's important for us to socialize there. He says it's good for his practice. Besides, I'm feeling tired these days."

Kim was most definitely on the defensive. Jennifer decided it was best not to press the subject. She planned on talking to Bob about Kim that evening.

A few minutes after Kim had hung up the phone, it rang again. This time it was John. "How about dinner at the club tonight at eight o'clock?"

"John, I'm really dragging today. Do you think you can go without me?"

"Of course not. You're my biggest asset. You charm the socks off those people. Take a nap this afternoon, and I'll see you this evening. And Kim, don't be late. It doesn't look good."

Kim hung up the phone and broke into tears. The past months with John had been one whirlwind of meaningless social engagements with people she didn't care about. Social climbing had never been of importance to her. She'd always had a comfortable niche in life and never had to push to make friends.

It wasn't so with John. He went at it as if it were a battle campaign, planning his strategy and the next conquest with military precision. One week it was the president of a bank, the next, the chairman of the board of the hospital. It's not that they weren't nice people, it's just that they weren't Kim's type. It was as if John was purposely cutting her off from family and old friends. She felt isolated, a prisoner in her own home.

She couldn't complain about her physical surroundings. Whether John had rented their apartment to provide her with a good home or to impress his new "friends" wasn't entirely clear to Kim. When they'd first married he seemed so solicitous and sincere. But she knew him much better now and didn't trust much of what he said.

Kim knew John's frequent calls were really to keep a check up on her whereabouts. It was an intolerable situation, but it was too late to pull out now. Her baby just had to have a legitimate father, not only for its sake, but for Bob and Jennifer's as well. Kim vowed to make the best of it for all their sakes, and began dressing for dinner.

It was a beautiful early June morning, one of the rare and wonderful days when everything on the universe seemed to be in tune. A shower the evening before had cleared the air of humidity, and the world seemed to sparkle fresh and clean in the sunlight. Jennifer was feeling fine, her pregnancy progressing well. Everything seemed to be going perfectly for a change.

Bob had a staff meeting at C.C.U., but even the thought of another bout with John Dixon couldn't spoil his happy mood. He wondered how Kim could stand the man, but to his surprise, they seemed to be doing just fine. *Maybe John has a good part I never see*, he thought as he got into the car.

"Damn!" Bob muttered as he approached Memorial. "I forgot to pick up those things for Jenny." He looked at his watch. "If I rush, I can get them and still get to the meeting in time." He speeded up and headed just a few blocks off his route to downtown. It only took a few minutes to pick up the items she'd ordered.

After a quick glance at the time, he rushed for the car, which was parked at a meter across the street. As Bob stepped out from the curb a van which had run the stop light at the corner, speeded toward him.

"Watch out!" a pedestrian shouted. But it was too late. The van hit Bob before he took the next step.

"It's too early for Bob to be calling," Jennifer thought as she picked up the phone. She'd expected him for lunch, but it wasn't unusual for him to call and cancel. A doctor's time was never truly his own, and having been married to two prominent physicians, Jennifer had no illusions about their priorities.

"I'm trying to locate a Mrs. Hughes," the emotionless voice on the phone said.

"This is she," Jennifer said apprehensively. Something about the voice made her nervous.

"There's been an accident."

"He's in intensive care, Mrs. Hughes," the nurse in emergency said. "I think you'd better speak to Dr. Stewart before you try to see him."

"Have his parents been notified?" Jennifer asked,

realizing Nancy and Chris should be there.

"Not yet. Dr. Stewart told us to have you wait for him here."

"I'm going to make a call and be right back," Jennifer said, forcing herself to remain calm. She'd been a nurse long enough to know that panic didn't accomplish anything. *Keep your head, Jenny*, she told herself. *He's in good hands here at Memorial.*

Jennifer could barely hold her tears back. She had to force herself to be calm before speaking to Nancy. "Mom," she said, trying to find the words to tell Bob's parents of the accident. "Mom. . . ." her voice cracked and she took a deep breath.

"Jennifer," Nancy said. "What's wrong? You sound absolutely—"

Jennifer forced the words out. "Mom. It's Bob! There's been an accident."

"How serious," Nancy asked.

"I don't know yet. He's in intensive care. I think you and Chris better get to Memorial as soon as possible."

"We'll be there as soon as possible, and Jennifer . . ."

"Yes," she answered, trying to keep from crying.

"Everything will be all right, dear."

"I want to believe that," Jennifer said, bursting into tears. When Dan approached Jennifer he was all business. The fact that she was a nurse, and a very good one, made it easier to be candid and professional. "Jennifer," Dan said. "We're doing all we can."

"How is he?" she asked.

Dan handed her a handkerchief to dry her tears. "I won't lie to you. He's in critical condition. The van was speeding and knocked him about ten feet. He landed on concrete. There's a head injury and some internal injuries as well. He's in a coma. As you know, that's not unusual in trauma cases. I expect he'll be coming around soon."

"May I see him?"

"Of course. But don't stay too long."

The intensive care unit at Memorial resembled the cardiac care unit to the point of where it would have been hard to tell them apart. To Jennifer it now seemed an entirely different place. She entered quietly, nodded to the nurse and went over to Bob. He was still. A bandage covered his head and one eye, and bruises showed on his cheek. There was an I.V. drip, and he was hooked up to vital sign monitors. It was so reminiscent of the scene of Sean's death that she almost wanted to run from the room.

"Bob," she whispered. "It's Jenny. I'm here now. I won't leave you." She knew he couldn't hear her, but the words were necessary, as much for her sake as for his.

Most of the members of Bob's family were gathered in the waiting room. Kim, worriedly ran over to Jennifer when she came out of intensive care. She told them what she knew, and tried to keep them calm, while inside, she wanted to scream.

Jennifer stared at Kim. "How did you know?"

"Nancy called me and told me what had happened. I knew you'd need me."

"Oh, Kim. I can't lose him. I love him so much . . ." She sobbed and Kim put an arm of comfort around her.

"I know," Kim said. "I know how much you love him, Jen. And he loves you. He told me so. Everything will be okay. It just has to be."

Jennifer realized Kim was stricken also. "I know you're very fond of Bob too," she said softly.

Kim didn't answer; she simply kept her arm around Jennifer, offering encouragement and telling herself that Jennifer must never know how much she really cared for Bob.

Even through her distress Jennifer noticed Kim looked pale and very tired. "Kim, I'm worried about you. Have you seen your doctor?" she asked.

"That's just like you, Jen. Worrying about everyone but yourself. You have Bob to worry about now. I'm just very tired."

"Is that all? You're sure."

"I'm sure," Kim assured her, knowing she hadn't told Jennifer the entire truth. She'd really been dragging lately, and now she felt slightly faint.

When Dan entered from I.C.U., Jennifer rushed up to him. "No change," he said. "Why don't you all go home. There's nothing you can do here. I'll call if there's anything."

"I want to be assigned here," Jennifer said.

"That's not a good idea," Dan said. "You're too close to him. And you're pregnant. It's much too much of a strain."

"I'll go crazy if I can't be here," she said. "Dan, I'll be a basket case if I can't be with him. I'll take the graveyard shift. It's hardest to get nurses then."

"Jennifer," Nancy said, taking her arm and leading her away. "You must rest. For both Bob and the baby's sake. It won't do any good to wear yourself out. There are plenty of competent nurses available."

"No," Jennifer said. "I won't leave him. I might as well be useful."

Seeing that Jennifer wouldn't relent, Dan thought it best to give in to her so as not to put any extra strain on her.

Jennifer went home, showered and changed and returned to the hospital immediately. She took over as Bob's nurse at midnight.

The room was dead quiet. Jennifer went over the chart, noting the medication and procedures Dan had prescribed, and then sat down by her husband's bedside.

"Bob. Oh, Bob, you've just got to be all right. You've just got to live to see our baby."

His eyelids fluttered and his lips parted. *Maybe if I keep talking to him, he'll come out of it,* she thought.

"Bob I love you. For the sake of the baby . . ."

"Baby . . ." Bob's head tossed, his eyelids fluttered again. He was coming out of the coma and was delirious. Jennifer leapt up and called Dan to inform him of the change. Since it was the middle of the night, he'd gone home and she knew it would take some time for him to get back to Memorial. In the meantime, it was best to keep Bob stimulated so he wouldn't lapse back into the coma.

"The baby . . ." Bob said.

"Yes, our baby, Bob," Jennifer whispered.

"Kim." Bob mumbled in his delirium.

Jennifer cocked her head and wondered why he had mentioned her sister. "It's Jenny, Bob."

In his delirium, Bob's mind wandered. The sisters fused, became interchangeable. "Kim—Are you all right? I'm sorry Kim. I loved you . . . The baby . . . Not John's—mine, Kim. It's my child . . . It's ours . . .

Can't hurt Jennifer. Can't tell her . . ."

Jennifer put her hand to her mouth, trying to keep back her cry as she realized what he was saying.

Bob began tossing wildly, mumbling about Kim and the baby. She had to calm him, to keep him from further injuring himself. Jennifer was crushed, but Bob needed her now even more than ever. She had to be strong for both of them.

"It's all right, Bob," Jennifer whispered. "It's all right. Jennifer doesn't know."

"Our secret," he murmured. "Our secret, Kim. Yours and mine . . ."

Jennifer brushed back a tear. "It will be our secret Bob. No one will ever know," she murmured.

"No one will ever know I know," Jennifer whispered to herself.

With her comforting words, Bob calmed and his breathing eased.

Dan arrived and examined Bob. "We're lucky," he said. "He's going to be fine. It's going to take a long recovery period, but it looks good."

Jennifer called Chris and Nancy to tell them the good news. She was exhausted.

I love Bob so much, she thought. *I just never could lose him. I don't know what I would have done if he'd died.*

She looked down at Bob, sleeping peacefully now, and bent to kiss him.

His eyes opened. "Jenny?"

"Yes, Bob, Jenny."

His eyes closed again and he smiled as he slept

Jennifer sat beside him, holding his hand. *You must never know I know about you and Kim. You must never know I know she's carrying your child. You both tried to*

181

spare me the hurt. I can't let this destroy either of you. I love you both too much. I forgive you Bob, and Kim too. How could she help but love you? But no one could love you as much as I do. No one ever can.

The house was very quiet when John arrived home from the hospital. "Kim," he called. "Kim. Where are you?"

He went into the bedroom to see if she was napping. He expected her to be there but she wasn't.

Having been through just a few months of pregnancy with her, John was glad he'd never chosen obstetrics as a specialty. He couldn't imagine himself putting up with all of that female nonsense. It wasn't like Kim to be gone so late. Usually, dinner was on the table and she was on the couch reading. He wondered where she'd gone.

John didn't like his routine disturbed. He liked having his meals ready, and being pampered. He resented Kim's being gone. Hungry, he opened the refrigerator, nibbling on some leftover turkey. When he heard the door open, he ran into the living room.

"Kim, where the hell have you been?"

"I've been visiting Bob at the hospital. I met Jennifer there, and we had a cup of tea in the cafeteria before I started home."

"You know how I like you to be here when I come home."

"Yes, but I haven't seen Bob in days."

"Yeah, well I don't care if you ever see him. He's not exactly my friend, you know."

"I wish you two would stop your feuding. It's so unproductive and hurtful."

"You don't know what you're talking about," John said, turning his back and putting on the TV news. "What's for dinner?"

"I'm really bushed. Why don't we send out. As a matter of fact, I'm not hungry at all. Just order something for yourself."

"Kim, the least you can do is fix a meal for your husband."

"It won't hurt you to get off your duff and help once in a while, John Dixon. I'm your wife, not your slave."

"Don't talk to me like that," John said, his face reddening. "Remember, I did you a favor by marrying you."

"I thought so at the time," Kim said. "I know better now. I'm your bid for social acceptance. You certainly don't have the personality to win over a flea."

His slap sent her reeling.

They'd argued many times before and Kim was aware he'd come close to hitting her several times. But this was the first time he'd actually done it.

"I'm giving Bob Hughes's bastard a name. Don't you forget that."

Kim suppressed her tears and lashed out in anger. "I know why you married me, John. It was to control me. To get hold of Bob's child so that you could lord it over both of us."

"What if I did. There's nothing you can do about it now. So, get dinner and shut up."

Kim caught her breath. The room was spinning and she wasn't sure she could get up if she tried. The trip to the hospital had exhausted her. Rather than let her sister know how badly she was feeling, she had pushed herself to get out of the house. What she wanted and needed more than anything else at that moment was to lie down and rest. But with John standing over her, Kim forced herself to move. She staggered toward the kitchen.

Kim reached for a saucepan and felt a twinge in her abdomen. She'd been spotting for days and hadn't said anything to anyone but Dr. Stratton. He'd told her that rest was essential. She hadn't wanted to tell John there was a problem with the pregnancy, and certainly didn't want to worry Jennifer, especially with Bob still so ill. Kim felt very weak and sat down to catch her breath. Then another pain, sharper than the one before shot through her midsection. She gasped and caught her breath before calling out.

"John!" He didn't come. Another pain and she doubled over. "John!"

Still angry, John strolled into the kitchen. "Yeah, now what—"

She had dropped to the floor. Blood stained the shining tile. She gasped the words. "Call Dr. Stratton. . . ."

John rushed to her. "Oh, my God! Kim, I'm sorry."

"Call the doctor, John, and call Jen."

He called Stratton and then an ambulance. He'd worry about Jennifer later.

John couldn't wait for Dr. Stratton to finish examining Kim. Instead, he barged into the room demanding a progress report immediately.

"John," Stratton said, pushing him out the door. "Husbands just don't belong here when their wives are having this kind of problem."

"But I can assist."

"You certainly can, by getting out of here and letting

me do my job."

"What caused—"

"I don't know yet. Now get out of here."

John had finally called Jennifer, and she'd joined him in the waiting room outside of the emergency room.

"What happened?" Jennifer asked. She remembered how weak Kim had looked that afternoon and felt terrible about not noticing she was in trouble.

"She was in the kitchen and called for me. By the time I got there, she'd collapsed."

"The baby?"

"I don't know. Stratton won't let me in there."

"Wise," Jennifer whispered.

"What's that?"

"I said it was wise of him. I've done enough nursing to know fathers are the last persons to allow in at such times."

"Oh," he said, his suspicions allayed.

When Dr. Stratton came out of the room, his expression told them everything. "I'm sorry, but the baby was already gone when she was brought in. It was a precarious pregnancy from the outset."

"She never told me," John said guiltily. He remembered the hard slap he'd given her that evening.

"No, John. She told me she didn't want to worry you."

"I'm her husband. I had a right to know there was a problem."

"That's between the two of you," Stratton said, wondering why Kim had been so adamant about keeping her condition from John.

"Can I see her now?" John asked.

Stratton's face darkened. "John, she doesn't want to

see you."

"She what?"

"Let her rest tonight. This isn't an unusual reaction. Often when a woman loses a child, particularly one she wants very much, she can't immediately face her husband. Time remedies it. Don't worry."

"How is she, Doctor," Jennifer asked.

"Despondent. Groggy. She'll recover fully in time. I gave her something for sleep. I think it would help if you went in for a few minutes. She asked for you."

Hospitals are rumor mills and there was no keeping the news of Kim's miscarriage from Bob. It was hard for him to hide his real feelings when he was told. All he could think about was Kim.

He felt the loss desperately and knew he had to see her, to share her grief, to let her know she wasn't alone.

It was after visiting hours when Bob convinced a nurse to wheel him to Kim's room. He had inquired after John and was told he'd left the hospital. That was good. John was the last person they needed to intrude upon them now.

Kim's face was turned away from the door when Bob entered. When the wheelchair bumped against the doorway she turned to see him. Tears streaked her cheeks. Her dark hair against the pillow framed her pale face.

"Bob," she said in surprise. "I didn't expect—"

Bob asked the nurse to leave them alone. When she'd gone, he took Kim's hand. "I couldn't let you go through this alone."

"I'm so sorry, I'm so sorry," she kept repeating the words over and over again. "I've lost our child . . ."

"It's not your fault," Bob said, stroking her hair. "These things happen. You'll have other children."

"Not yours, my love." She pulled her hand from his. "This is our punishment."

"Kim, you can't believe that."

"It's retribution for our betrayal of Jennifer. Our baby was the sacrifice."

"No. No. Kim, you mustn't feel that way."

"Do you forgive me?"

"Forgive you? I'm the one that needs forgiving. I abandoned you and the child."

"No! Bob. No! There was no choice. For Jennifer's sake, you had no choice."

He could see she was tiring and was just about to break. "Kim, I'll always love you. Please, forgive yourself. You'll tear yourself apart like this. I couldn't live with that."

She made a slight attempt to smile. "I'll be okay. Bob. Please don't try to see me again."

It was not the time to upset her further with an argument. Bob leaned over Kim and gently kissed her lips.

With tears burning in her eyes, she turned away.

It was early July now, the dog days of the midwestern summer had taken hold. For a short time John had become kind and helpful, but as her condition improved, his disposition worsened. He was soon the old John she'd come to know and hate, as selfish and demanding as ever.

Kim was waiting for John in the living room when he arrived home from the hospital one evening. She was dressed in a white tailored linen suit and a navy straw hat. Her bags were in the entry, packed and ready to go.

John nearly tripped over them as he came in through the door. "What's this?" He said, skirting the bags. "Are we going somewhere?"

"I'm leaving you, John," Kim said, pushing past him. "I just wanted to tell you that to your face."

"Hey, wait a minute. You're not going anywhere, my dear."

"You can't stop me. If you hit me, I'll . . ."

John laughed. "I don't have to hit you. You won't leave me. I guarantee it."

"You have nothing to hold me anymore," Kim said. "The baby's gone. Our marriage is a farce."

"That's not what everyone else thinks."

"I don't care what everyone else thinks. I just can't stay with you one more minute. You're a monster, John. Everything you ever do is motivated by selfishness. I can't think of one thing you've done out of compassion or love."

"I've learned those qualities don't get you very far in this world," he said.

She opened the door to leave.

John smiled. "I suppose you'd like Jennifer to know who the father of your bastard really was," he said coldly.

She stopped short. "John, you wouldn't!"

His smiled broadened. "Oh, wouldn't I now? Try me!" He reached for the phone.

Kim knew he had defeated her. She couldn't permit John to tell Jennifer that Bob was the father of her dead child. She couldn't let him hurt her sister that much. She felt she alone should pay for what she'd done.

Unaware that Jennifer already knew the truth and

had forgiven her, Kim relented. "You win, John," she said, closing the door behind her. "I'll stay with you as long as you don't tell Jennifer."

He came over to Kim and kissed her hard on the mouth. "You see, one way or another, I always get what I want."

The evening was chilly for October. Halloween candy lined the shelves of the grocery stores, and fat orange pumpkins brightened corner lots. Soon, little ghosts and goblins would be running down the street. And tonight, Bob and Jennifer's child was due.

Kim looked out the window and smiled to herself. At least Jennifer and Bob were happy. That was worth her sacrifice.

The moon was a crescent in the sky, and the stars were bright overhead. Lights in the houses cast warm shadows on the street. Jennifer and Bob strolled, hand in hand, enjoying the slight nip in the air and the beauty of the evening.

"I love you so much it hurts," he said, nuzzling her neck.

"And I love you. You can't know how much. To think I nearly lost you."

"You'll never lose me," Bob said, stopping under the streetlamp. "You're beautiful you know. That little girl of ours is going to have hair just like yours. She's going to be just like her lovely mother."

"What if it's a boy?"

"I think I could go for that," Bob said, kissing her again. "As long as he's a part of you and me."

A shooting star streaked across the darkened sky. Bob

looked up and pointed. "That's ours, Jenny. God's fireworks. Even the sky is celebrating our love."

They walked together under the evening sky and shared a universe of love.

How to Win Big Prizes

You can now order previous titles of *Soaps & Serials*™ Books by mail!

Just complete the order form, detach, and send together with your check or money order payable to:

Soaps & Serials™
120 Brighton Road, Box 5201
Clifton, NJ 07015-5201

- -

Please <u>circle</u> the book #'s you wish to order:

The Young and The Restless	1	2	3	4	5
Days of Our Lives	1	2	3	4	5
Guiding Light	1	2	3	4	5
Another World	1	2	3	4	5
As The World Turns	1	2	3	4	5
Capitol™	1	2	3	4	
Dallas™	1	2	3	4	5
Knots Landing™	1	2	3	4	5

Each book is $2.50 ($3.25 in Canada).

Total number of books
circled _____ × price above = $ _____ .

Sales tax (CT and NY residents only) $ _____ .

Shipping and Handling $ _____ .95

Total payment enclosed $ _____ .
(check or money orders only)

Name _____

Address _____ Apt# _____

City _____

State _____ Zip _____

Telephone (_____) _____
　　　　Area code　　　　　　　　　　　　　　ATWT5

Soaps & Serials™ Fans!

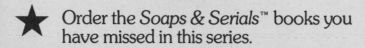

★ Order the *Soaps & Serials*™ books you have missed in this series.

★ Collect other *Soaps & Serials*™ series from their very beginnings.

★ Give *Soaps & Serials*™ series as gifts to other fans.

...see other side for ordering information